Daddy Dom 5

Paul's Perfect Princess

+

Daddy's Assistant

A DDLG and ABDL 2 in 1 novel collection

of kinky BDSM age play stories

By Tina Moore

Table of Contents

Paul's Perfect Princess

A DDLG and ABDL romantic age play love story about an unlikely Daddy Dom finding his perfect baby girl

By Tina Moore

Chapter 1

Hannah frantically read over her notes in the break room, reviewing them again and again as if she hadn't long ago memorized the information. Claire watched her with amusement as Hannah muttered under her breath from time to time and chewed on her finger anxiously.

"I wouldn't so blatant about that if I were you," Claire chimed in. "Mr. Williams would blow a fuse if he saw you studying on company time." Hannah looked up at her, so focused on the task at hand that it took several moments for the words to register.

"Huh? Oh, I was just going over these notes one last time. My last final is at four o'clock this afternoon and traffic is so bad this time of day. I don't think I'll have time for any last-minute cramming after work, so I'm trying to fit it all in now."

"What are you so worried about anyway? You know all of this by heart. You've done nothing but live, eat, and breathe Marine Biology since I met you. You should be enjoying your upcoming freedom. You're going to ace this test just like you've aced every test since I've known you. So relax a little already. Haven't you ever heard of senioritis?"

"I'll relax once I've graduated," Hannah muttered. Claire looked at her through narrow eyes.

"Is that so? I'll remember that you said that. I know of a couple of really good parties going on next weekend."

"Wait. What? No, I didn't mean it like that. "Claire was always trying to drag her to some party or another, but Hannah always declined. Between work and school, she just didn't have time for any kind of socializing. Even if she did have the time, she hated parties, preferring to get together with small groups of friends rather than the kinds of parties that Claire liked to attend. Crowds made her nervous, and she could never relax enough to enjoy herself if there were too many people and a bunch of loud noises. Mr. Williams came in and hurriedly made a beeline for the coffee pot. Hannah felt like she had been saved by the bell until she remembered that she was on the clock. She jumped to hide her notes before he noticed them, shoving them awkwardly in her bathing suit. As he turned around and nodded at the girls in greeting, he did a double-take at the strange, crumpled lump under Hannah's suit but only shook his head. Hannah did her best to behave as though nothing was amiss.

"Claire, your tour group, has arrived, you had better get out there." He took a loud slurp of his coffee and leaned against the counter.

"Sure thing, Mr. Williams," she said with a fake cheeriness and left. Hannah hated it when she did that; it was so awkward. She could never tell if Mr. Williams didn't realize that she was being sarcastic or if he just didn't care. Both seemed equally as likely.

"Hey, don't you have a big test today or something?" he asked, loudly slurping on his coffee once again. It was such an annoying habit that set Hannah's teeth on edge.

"My last final. It all comes down to this." She felt her stomach tighten, her nervousness coming back full force. It wasn't the information that was going to be on the final that had her so anxious but rather the finality of it all. Four years of working toward a singular goal, and she was finally within sight of the finish line. All she had to do was try not to fall flat on her face. Right. No problem. She chewed on her lip again, feeling a raw spot starting to form there.

"Well, good luck and try not to get too in your head about it, you don't want to get the yips. Hey, why don't you take off early today since there are no more tour groups scheduled? I expect it will be pretty quiet around here for the rest of the day. If there are any last-minute bookings, Claire can handle it."

"Oh, thank you so much, Mr. Williams!" she said, a wave of relief washing over her. "I really needed that extra time to study."

"Oh, you'll do fine, you're a smart kid. Now go knock 'em dead." Hannah was so grateful that she hugged the man before rushing off the locker room. She grabbed her bag and slipped on a pair of jean shorts and a t-shirt over her bathing suit, not willing to spare the time it would take to change. She waited until she got to her car before pulling the crumpled notes out of her bathing suit. They were a little damp but still readable. She smoothed them out on the steering wheel, looking them over again before heading to class. In truth, she really did know all of this information front and backward, but going over her notes soothed her nerved. As she tried to crank her car, however, there was only a terrible sound of metal grinding on metal before it went dead again. She tried to turn the engine again, but the grinding sound only got worse, followed by a plume of black smoke that came out from under the hood. So much for her nerves. Hannah cursed and popped the hood, getting out of the car in a huff, despairing that this would happen at such an inconvenient moment. She tried to pry the hood the rest of the way open, but the metal was hot to the touch, and she jerked her hand away with another curse. Tears of pain and frustration sprung to her eyes, and she could feel panic beginning to rise in her throat, feeling at a total loss. Should she call a mechanic first or a cab first? It was so hard to think straight with her heart pounding.

"Whoa, there, pretty lady," she heard a deep voice behind her say. She turned to find the most handsome man she had ever seen approaching her. As he got closer, she recognized him as Paul Peterson: local celebrity, professional surfer, and an all-around popular party guy. Hannah had seen him at the beach pretty frequently, practicing his moves and flirting with the girls that were always flocking around him. He was hard not to notice, classically handsome, charismatic, incredibly fit. He had shiny black hair, brown eyes, and a broad frame. She had never even considered trying to talk to him before. He seemed like he was from another world and she was content to watch him from afar.

"Need a hand?" asked Paul. She instantly felt a jolt of attraction as their eyes met, making her legs feel a bit wobbly all of a sudden. She had only ever seen him from across the beach or on local television. Up close and in person was a whole other ballgame. He looked her up and down appraisingly, then smiled in a way that made it obvious that he liked what he saw, and she could feel her body responding to him despite the stressful situation.

"Um, yeah, I guess I do," she said, feeling a bit dazed. The car trouble suddenly seemed even more annoying because she had to focus on that when she would rather be flirting with this handsome gentleman.

"What seems to be the problem?" he asked. Again, she felt a tingling heat come over her as she stared into his eyes, dumbstruck for a moment.

She tore her eyes away from him reluctantly and looked at the smoking wreckage that had been a functioning vehicle just that morning.

"Um, I'm really not sure, it just started doing this just now," she said. The panic came rushing back, and she was sure that he could hear it in her voice. "I don't know a thing about cars, unfortunately, so I really don't have a clue what could be wrong with it."

"Ok, well, don't worry, miss," said Paul, flashing the brightest smile at her that she had ever seen. "It just so happens that I'm friends with the best mechanic in town. I can give him a call if you'd like, ask him to send a wrecker out and take a look at it."

"No," she said, shaking her head. "That's too much. I couldn't ask you to do that."

"You didn't ask," he retorted with a wink. "And neither did I. There is no way that I'm leaving a pretty lady as you stranded here like this." She found herself blushing and annoyed at the same time, a strange combination. The wild roller coaster of emotions had left her feeling on edge.

"So if I weren't pretty, you would leave me stranded here?" she asked, putting her hands on her hips. He laughed, throwing his head back. The sunlight glinted off his shiny black hair, and all trace of annoyance disappeared instantly. How could anyone ever be annoyed at such beauty?

"Of course not," he said, still chuckling. "I just wanted an excuse to let you know that you're pretty."

"Oh," she said, feeling suddenly chagrined. "I don't need you to tell me I'm pretty. I already know that." She said with an unimpressed look. She must have dropped one of her notecards because Paul spotted one of her them being blown away by the wind and chased it down with feline grace and speed.

"Is this yours?" he asked, handing it to her.

"Oh no! I'm going to be so late for my final!" She mentally kicked herself for spending her time flirting with him when she had real problems to deal with.

"When and where is it?" asked Paul.

"It's not far, luckily, and it doesn't start for another couple of hours, but who knows how long it will take to get the wrecker out here! And then I'll have to get a cab! Oh no, I'm really going to be late." Her voice got more and more frantic as she listed off her problems. Paul shook his head and fished his car keys out of his pocket.

"No, you don't need to worry about any of that. You just worry about passing your final. How about I'll trade you my car for yours. Let me take care of your car. You can get mine back to me in a few days."

"But, how will you get around?" she asked reluctantly. She couldn't just take this guy's car, could she? They had only known each other for a couple of minutes.

"I have another one," said Paul shrugging. "I'll take an Uber home and drive my other car until yours is fixed." He pulled a business card out from his wallet. "Text your name to this number. What is your name, by the way?"

"Hannah," she said quietly, taking the card.

"I'm having a party tomorrow night at my place. You should hang out, have a few drinks. It will be fun!" Hannah nodded slowly as they shoved the keys into her hands. He put a hand on the small of her back and started guiding her towards her car. That small, subtly dominant touch set her inner core on fire, and she was suddenly finding it very hard to think.

"Are you sure you want just to give me your car? You just met me. I could be some sleazy dirtbag who's going to take your car and sell it on the black market for all you know." Again, he laughed making Hannah blush even deeper. Surely the idea of her being a criminal wasn't that laughable.

"I am absolutely certain. The only thing I want you worrying about right now is your test. Promise?"

"Ok," she sighed. "I guess that I'm not really in a position to argue." Paul was opening the driver's side door for her and shooing her into the vehicle.

"You'd better get going now. I'll see you tomorrow at the party tomorrow night."

"Ok, I'll see you there." For a moment, she could only watch him and wondered what the heck had just happened before she came back to herself and put the car in drive. She did her best to put his handsome face out of her mind and focus.

Chapter 2

Hannah was already at work when Claire dragged herself in the next morning, looking like hell had warmed over. Hannah had been pouring herself a cup of coffee and after one look at Claire, poured her a cup as well.

"Rough night?" she asked as she slid the cup across the counter. Claire nodded and gratefully took several deep gulps from the mug before coming up for air, giving a big satisfied sigh.

"Yes, I was partying really late last night. Thank you so much for the coffee. I really needed that. Oh hey, how did the test go?" she asked, swatting Hannah playfully on the arm.

"Ugh, I think I did, OK. I second-guessed myself on a lot the answers and spent so long debating if it was right or not that I ran out of time. They won't post my grades for a few days, so I'll just have to wait until then to find out." Hannah's face twisted, thinking about how fraught with anxiety she would be over the next few days. She didn't think it would be possible to concentrate on anything else.

"I still don't get why you're so freaked out. Even if you totally bombed it, which I doubt, there's no way you could fail with such a high GPA, right?"

"Yeah, that's true," Hannah sighed. "But I wouldn't be able to graduate with honors."

"Oh," Claire said, nodding slowly. "I guess that is a pretty big deal. But, hey, what's done is done, and I am sure you did fine. You are by far the smartest person I know. And no matter what happens with this test, you are finally done. Done with school and studying and all-nighters followed by early morning shifts, done with being permanently exhausted. I say that calls for a celebration." Hannah laughed at the coincidence.

"It's funny. You should mention that. You've heard of Paul Peterson, right?" Claire nodded impatiently. Of course, she had, everyone around here knew who he was.

"Well, he's throwing a party this evening at his beach house, and he invited me." Claire nearly choked on her coffee at that revelation.

"What?!" she screeched. "He invited you personally? Why didn't you lead with that? When did you meet him?"

"Yesterday," Hannah confessed. "I had a little car trouble on my way to my test, and he rescued me."

"What, like he helped you change your flat tire? That's so hot. Did he take his shirt off like in the movies?" Claire's enthusiasm was so infectious that Hannah laughed, blushing slightly at the image. Suddenly she wished that he had taken off his shirt.

"No, it was a lot worse than a flat tire. He had to call a wrecker. It was so bad. I was freaking out about being late for my test, and Paul just let me borrow his car." Claire's eyebrows shot up.

"What? He just gave you his car? He must

want you pretty bad."

"What, me? Why would you say that? Maybe he's just a nice guy. He has plenty of money, I'm sure. He's constantly winning surfing championships and getting endorsement deals."

"Rich or not, nice guys don't just go around handing over their cars to strange women that they just met. That dude wants to put it in you."

"Claire!" she gasped. "That's so crass!" Claire just shrugged and grinned, unrepentant.

"The truth is the truth. I might not be as smart as you, but I know men. Snap him up while you can. You are going to the party, right? I know it isn't your usual thing, but you absolutely cannot miss this. How often do rich handsome men invite you over to party with them?"

"Yes, I'm going. I'm supposed to give the car back to him then so I pretty much have to. I'm nervous about going, though. You know how much I hate parties."

"Don't look at it as a party; look at it as a networking opportunity. You're a recent college graduate about to enter the workforce. You need to get out there and meet some of the folks in the community instead of hiding behind a book all the time." Hannah had to admit that Claire had a good point there. She wasn't originally from the island and didn't actually know many people. If she wanted to stay here and get a job, which she did, she would have to get out there and meet someone whose aunt's neighbor or whatever had an in with a local aquarium or conservation group. Hannah had been too busy for an internship, having to spend all of her free time working someplace that could pay, and that meant she was already a step behind most of the other graduates in the marine biology program. She sighed in defeat, knowing it was unavoidable. Claire squealed with delight and did a happy little dance.

"Excellent, what time are you going?"

"It starts at eight."

"Don't you dare show up before nine-thirty. Oh, and you had better wear something slutty." Hannah blushed and crossed her arms over her chest self-consciously.

"I most certainly will not," she said indignantly. "How would that help my chances of getting a job?" Claire scoffed.

"That's not what I'm worried about. You need to get laid, like yesterday." Hannah's blush deepened to her chest, wondering what had brought on such crass language all of a sudden. Claire knew how much she hated that.

"Claire!" she hissed, embarrassed.

"What?!" asked Claire innocently. "I don't think I've ever even heard you mention a date, much less a boyfriend. You need some companionship, the touch of another human being, or I swear to god you're going to pop like a little overworked, undersexed balloon."

"Whatever," muttered Hannah, hoping to drop the conversation before she died of embarrassment. Claire picked up her mug of coffee and headed toward the break room door to start her day. She paused by the door, giving Hannah one last word of advice before she left.

"Slutty," she said pointedly and let the door swing shut behind her.

Chapter 3

Hannah parked Paul's car at the address he had texted her. She may not know much about cars, but this one was obviously much nicer than hers, and she was going to miss having heated seats and windows you didn't have to crank open by hand. There were a bunch of people out on the front lawn, drinking and talking. Hannah didn't see anyone she recognized, but that was to be expected. She went in and did a lap around the house looking for Paul, but she didn't see him yet, so she passed the time admiring the house instead. It was a modern design with lots of light-colored wood and an open airy floor plan. It was the perfect beach house. She reflected as she examined the built-in bookshelves and wondered how much the whole thing cost. To her surprise, the books were a little higher brow than she expected. She felt a pang of guilt at the thought, knowing that she really shouldn't stereotype people. Just because they were surfers didn't mean they weren't perfectly intelligent. Still, she honestly didn't expect to come across an extensive science fiction collection. She saw a book by an author she had been meaning to check but hadn't gotten around to yet. She took one last look around the room for Paul and, when she didn't see him, slipped the book into her bag and went upstairs. There were some empty bedrooms up there, and she picked the one that looked the most like a guest room. She didn't want to violate anyone's privacy. She just wanted a quiet place to read and escape the crowd for a while. She sat in a chair next to a desk, one foot tucked under her, and turned on the desk lamp. Soon, she was completely engrossed in the story and completely lost track of time and what she was supposed to be doing. Some time into the third chapter, she heard the door creak open and looked up to see Paul.

"Oh, hello!" he said good-naturedly, looking

surprised yet very happy to see her. "Did you get lost?"

"Not exactly," Hannah said shyly. "I just wanted to find a quiet spot, and it didn't seem like anyone was using this room at the moment. Sorry if I bothered something."

"You're not bothering a thing, pretty lady. What book do you have there?" He looked a little closer and nodded approvingly. "A woman of refined tastes, I see. That is one of my personal favorites." Paul was wearing a pair of distressed khakis and a green button-up that complimented his chocolate eyes and dark features perfectly. It gave him a slightly more refined air, a side of him she had no idea existed.

"You know you look a lot different when you're not on the beach," she said.

"Let me guess. You almost didn't recognize me with my shirt on?" She blushed which only made him laugh harder. It was an infectious laugh, and Hannah found herself smiling despite her faux pas.

"I guess you get that a lot, huh?" she asked, hoping that at least she wasn't the only one.

"Oh, all the time. It's kind of nice actually, almost like having a secret identity. Shirtless Surfer Man by day and boring old Paul by night."

"I've only just met you, but it's hard to imagine you being boring." It came out of her mouth before she even realized how flirty is sounded. "I mean, your book collection alone is fascinating." Somehow that last part sounded even more flirty. She tried not to blush again but was sure that she was failing.

"Why, thank you. You can take that home with you if you like. Just bring it back by anytime when you're finished." He winked at her when he said that last part and Hannah wondered if he was flirting back or just being friendly. She had never been able to tell the difference until they were directly asking her out.

"You're so kind. Oh, that reminds me, here are your keys back. I can't thank you enough for letting me borrow it." He only shook his head and waved them away.

"I'm afraid your car won't be ready for a couple more days. My mechanic friend says he will have to order a part from the mainland, and you know how long that can take. You hold on to those for a few more days. Why are you up here all alone?" he asked abruptly, changing the subject, interrupting her objections before she could give them.

"Oh, I just got a little overwhelmed by the crowd. I don't know anyone, and parties make me nervous." She cringed inside, wondering what kind of boring wallflower she was sounding like to this handsome, charming, social butterfly.

"To tell you the truth," he leaned in conspiratorially. "Parties make me nervous too. I was actually slipping up here to escape the crowd as well. It's getting kind of crazy down there." She gave him a skeptical look, wondering if he was only humoring her.

"But this is your party. Why would you throw a party if they make you nervous?"

"It's good for business," he shrugged and walked over the window, looking out at the partygoers on the front yard. "Most endorsement deals happen because of who you know rather than what you can do. I'm relatively unknown in the sport at the moment, so I have to hustle a little harder. Besides, I know most of these people, some of them really well. That helps a lot. Would you like me to introduce you to some nice folks? It might make you feel a little less nervous." She bit her lip, wanting to stay in this nice quiet room with this nice handsome man, but she knew that she should suck it up and go make some new friends.

"Tell you what. We'll make the rounds for ten minutes. Then we can come back up here and take another breather. How does that sound?"

"Really? That's so sweet. Okay, yeah, let's do it." He motioned toward the door, indicating that she should go first. As she walked by, he put his hand on the small of her back, guiding her through the door as he held it open for her. She felt her heart fluttering at the romantic gesture. If was even meant to be romantic. Maybe he was just nice. Again, the old conundrum. They went downstairs, and Paul pulled a few people to the side to make introductions. She found herself answering the same questions over and over again. What do you do? Are you seeing anyone? Isn't Paul totally awesome? By the end of the ten minutes, her head was swimming. She didn't know how she was ever going to remember any of those names, and she was sure she would remember less than half of the faces. She felt Paul's hand on the small of her back again, leading her towards the stairs, and she let him lead her, grateful for the break.

"Well, that was a good round, I think," he said once they were back in their hiding spot. "We can go back down again later if you want. For now, I'd like to further make your acquaintance if I may." She noticed that he was looking at her expectantly. She suddenly felt a little overwhelmed by the attention. Such a handsome, kind man looking at her as though she were a tasty snack, it was almost too much.

"Well, sure, but I think you'll find that I'm rather boring." Paul shook his head. "I don't believe that for a second. Why would you say that?"

"All I do is work and study."

"What do you study?" asked Paul.

"I study Marine Biology, or at least I did. I took my last test today, and I'll graduate in a couple of weeks."

"Wow, that's amazing," said Paul. "It must have been really difficult to put yourself through school like that. That's quite an accomplishment. Although if you work down at the marina, I'm surprised I haven't seen you before yesterday. I'm there all the time."

"I've seen you," she shrugged. "But, there's usually a bit of a crowd around you."

"And you hate crowds," Paul laughed. "Still, I feel like I would have noticed you, even across a crowded beach. You're a very lovely woman,

Hannah." Hannah blushed yet again. She got the uncanny feeling that he was undressing her with his eyes, and she suddenly didn't know where to look or what to do with her hands. She tried to change the subject.

"Well, I'll be down there even more now that I'm done with school. I'll be doing dolphin tours full time now, I suppose."

"You don't have another job lined up yet? One closer to your field, I mean." She sighed and bit her lip before answering, not wanting to load this kind gentleman down with her sob story.

"No, I've put in a few applications but no callbacks yet. They give preference to people with internship experience, and I couldn't afford that. I just have to hope that they get desperate, and I get lucky." He looked thoughtful for a moment.

"If you'd like, I can make some inquiries around town. I know lots of folks in town. Surely some of them are looking for a capable yet beautiful Marine Biologist." Hannah's face lit up. She couldn't believe it. She had suddenly gone from having no leads to having the most influential person in town, offering his help. She wondered vaguely which lucky star she had to thank for this small miracle.

"Really, you would do that for me?" she gushed.

"Of course I would," said Paul. "I would love to help you." She was glowing from within, feeling very lucky indeed to have made such a wonderful friend. It was flattering, having the full attention of a man who was constantly surrounded by beautiful women. That he was willing to go so far out of his way for her was incredibly touching.

"As a matter of fact, I'm having another event the day after tomorrow, a surfing demo. Would you like to come? It probably won't be as crowded as the party tonight was."

"Ok," she said, trying to sound casual when really she was eager for a chance to see him again. "Yeah, I can try to make that. What time?"

"It starts at four," said Paul. "But if you can get there early, you can hang out with me in the 'green room' which in reality is really just a tent with a cooler. You in?"

"Yeah, I'll see if I can get off work a couple of hours early." He grinned, suddenly looking very proud of himself.

"Well, alright then, sounds like a date," said Paul, looking as happy as a clam. Hannah was certain that he didn't mean it the way that it sounded, but she blushed anyway. He wouldn't be interested in someone like her, would he? He did seem like he was flirting with her, but she couldn't see why he would like someone like her.

"Well, I guess I'd better take off," she said, beginning to feel the effects of the late hour and a long stressful week. He looked incredibly disappointed.

"So soon?" asked Paul, standing up from the desk. "Why don't you stay a bit longer? I could go get us some drinks." Hannah was tempted but only shook her head.

"No, it's getting pretty late for my tastes, to be honest, I'm somewhat of an early bird. And I have work again tomorrow."

"Well, alright, if you must you must," said Paul. He held out his hand for her to shake. As she took it, it was warm and engulfed her hand like she imagined a bear's paw would. Now that he was standing, she noticed how much taller than her he was, how he loomed over her, dominant energy coming off of him like waves. He shook her hand a couple of times, then raised it to his lips to kiss her knuckle reverently. He looked at her and winked before dropping her hand. "It was very nice to see you again, Hannah. I hope that we see each other again soon."

"Thank you," she said breathlessly. "I hope that we do, too. Thank you for a lovely evening. This is by far the best party I've ever been to." They both laughed and waved at one another as she edged her way reluctantly towards the door. She secretly wished that she could stay here for the rest of the night but was also afraid that she would blow it if she did. When she opened the door, the din of the party invaded their little sanctuary, breaking the magic that it seemed to hold. With one last wave over her shoulder, she left.

***

Paul tossed and turned all night, scarcely able to rid himself of the thoughts of Hannah that plagued even his dreams. How he longed to spread those perfect thighs and slide himself inside of her, to feel her squirm and moan beneath him, calling him Daddy as she wrapped herself around him and begged for more. Hannah was kind, smart, beautiful, and every part of him was on fire at the thought of her, and he had to possess her completely.

She's probably not a little, Paul warned himself. *She probably doesn't even know what it means. Don't get your hopes up.* Still, there was something about her that made him hopeful. Being a Daddy was hard sometimes. He longed for a real relationship, a baby girl that he could call his very own, but all of the women he'd dated were varying levels of disinterested or disgusted by his affinity. Paul sighed heavily, wishing he could dress Hannah up in pretty dresses, buy her all the toys her heart desired, and snuggle up next to her every night. Snuggling wasn't all he dreamed of doing to her. What he wouldn't give to hear her call him Daddy as he fucked her. The thought was too much, and he grasped his hard cock, desperate for relief. He stroked his cock feverishly, imagining it was Hannah's delicate pink lips wrapped around his hardness instead of his own hand. In his mind's eye, her cheeks were flushed pink after cumming like a good girl so many times on his cock that they both had lost count. Her eyes fluttered closed as she gripped his buttocks and bucked her hips against his, milking him with her tight little cunt.

"Cum for me, Daddy," she would whisper, and he would empty his load so deep inside of her. He grunted and soiled his sheets, cumming with a shuddering groan. He kicked his wet sheets to the floor, but it wasn't enough to relieve the tension.

Eventually, he fell into a fitful sleep, still whispering Hannah's name.

Chapter 4

Hannah put extra time into her hair and makeup the day of the demo, knowing that she was going to be seeing her new favorite guy. She picked out her cutest outfit, a dress that was tight enough to show off her curves but also concealed her diaper. She almost hadn't worn it, but she figured that if anything romantic did happen with Paul, she could just excuse herself to the bathroom and take it off. She had gotten very good at hiding this part of her life from romantic partners over the years. Secretly, she dreamed of finding a Daddy of her very own someday, someone to pamper her and take care of her, but for now she was content to keep her secret. Wearing a diaper soothed her nerves, and she was every bit as nervous as she was excited. Paul had been texting her all day, telling her how excited he was to see her, too. She followed his directions and found the place easily enough. It took her a few minutes of trying to calm the butterflies in her stomach before she could go in, however. Finally, she calmed herself enough to enter the tent. It was actually very nice inside, much more than "just a tent with a cooler" as he had so humbly put it. There was a DJ and a full bar, as well as a dozen or more people mingling around. The tent was large enough that it didn't seem at all crowded, something that put her a little more at ease. Paul spotted her around the same time, and she noticed that when he saw her, his face lit up. He quickly disentangled himself from his current conversation with a couple of guys in suits and rushed right over to her. He was in his swim trunks already, but blessedly he still had his t-shirt on. She was fairly certain that her head would literally explode if he came at her shirtless. It seemed as though Claire was right about her needing to get laid.

"Glad you could make it," he said slyly. The gleam in his chocolatey brown eyes told her that he was very glad indeed. The way he looked at her, raw hunger on his face, made her burn for him.

"Thank you for inviting me," she said, hoping that she wasn't blushing. "This is really great."

"Would you like a drink?" he asked.

"Yeah, a drink sounds really nice," she said. She was hoping that a little bit of liquid courage would loosen her up a bit. As he led her toward the bar, Paul put a hand on the small of her back, subtly maneuvering her. The gesture made her sweat a little, her heart suddenly beating faster. She ordered a beer, and he waved away her card, telling the bartender to put it on his tab.

"Are you kidding? You don't pay for anything when you're with me," he said with a wink and handed her the beer. She blushed and tried to hide it by taking a sip of the foamy beer.

"Thanks, that's really nice," she said once she had recovered a few her wits.

"Would you like me to introduce you around the room?" asked Paul, leaning in close to ask. The feel of his breath on her neck had her feeling a bit woozy.

"Maybe in a minute," she said, suddenly feeling like she might need to sit down. "But don't let me hold you back, you go ahead and mingle if you need to." He shook his head.

"Oh no, I'm not leaving your side until the event starts. Can't have some other guy come and snap you up now, can I?" She giggled at the unlikely though and sipped her beer again, trying to regain her composure. She didn't think there was a single man in the universe who could tear her away from Paul at that moment.

"Oh, that reminds me," Paul said. "You left that book behind the other night. You were only three chapters in, just wait until chapter eight, you won't believe it!"

"You've read it?"

"Of course! I've read the whole series dozens of times."

"That's really cool. Thanks for the reminder, I've been meaning to read more lately, especially now that I have more free time."

"Speaking of which, what are you doing after this?" asked Paul.

"Nothing. My boss gave me the whole day off work, so I'm totally free." She cringed inwardly, hoping that she didn't sound too overeager.

"Good," he said, a bit lower so no one would overhear. "I want to take you somewhere private after this." He was giving her that look again like he was undressing her with their eyes. She felt hot all over her body under his gaze.

"Where do you want to go?" It didn't really matter to her where they went. She had a feeling that she would follow him anywhere. Before he could answer, a very drunk guy in a black t-shirt came over and started gushing about what a big fan he was. Paul handled him graciously, signing autographs for him and taking selfies with him. The guy eventually went away happy, presumably to go get even drunker.

"Sorry about that," said Paul. "Look, I have to go get ready for this thing now, but it shouldn't take too long. Then I have a quick interview, but I'll do my best to speed through it. Would you mind waiting around for a while? It'll be worth it, I promise."

"Yeah, of course, I'll stick around. I'm really excited about seeing you surf finally. Everyone says you are the best."

"Why, thank you," he grinned. "Just stick to the tent. For now, no one should bother you here. They'll announce when I'm about to go out. Think you'll be OK on your own for a while?"

"Yeah, of course. I'll just hang here, and you can text me when you're done."

"OK, cool. I'll see you soon." He kissed her hand again before disappearing.

Chapter 5

The surfing demo was very interesting to watch. Paul did tricks and flips that Hannah had never even heard of before. Not that she knew much about surfing in the first place. She was a strong swimmer and boogie boarder but had never had the time or inclination to learn how to surf. Everyone in the crowd oohed and ahhed as he did his tricks, and Hannah felt very proud of her new friend. It was clear to her that he took his craft very seriously, something that only made him more attractive to her.

As she watched him in action, she pondered on their newfound friendship. There was an undeniable sexual chemistry between them, something that she found exciting but also confusing. Maybe she was misreading things, and what she had thought was flirtatious behavior was really just kindness. Maybe he just wanted to be friends. She hoped not, though, she realized as she watched his tanned muscular body move under the afternoon sun. Watching him being so physical made her want to get physical with him as well and not on a surfboard. It had been a while since she had met anyone that she was attracted to, but it was undeniable the way that this man-made her feel. It was intoxicating to imagine his hands on her, his lips kissing her neck and breasts. She even indulged herself by imagining calling him "Daddy" in her fantasy, hearing him whisper "baby girl" before he pulled her close for a passionate kiss.

As she was lost in her reverie, someone snatched her purse and ran off with it into the crowd. She snapped herself back to reality and called after the thief, crying out for someone to stop him, but he was gone in a flash before anyone could react. She tried combing through the crown but to no avail.

As she looked around at the sea of strange faces, she began to realize how screwed she actually was. Everything that she needed was in that bag.

She had been so concerned with looking cute that she had worn an outfit with no pockets. That meant her wallet, her cellphone, Paul's car keys, everything was now gone. As tears began to spring to her eyes, she noticed that people were beginning to look at her strangely which only made her more upset. She was sure that she looked like a crazy person, with panicked eyes and smeared mascara. She started pushing her way to the back of the crowd, wanting to get away and find a quiet place to think. She had no idea how she was going to get a hold of Paul or how she was going to get home. Once she did, how would she ever be able to tell Paul that she had lost his car keys after he had trusted her with them? Was their blossoming friendship already over before it had a chance to really begin? That last thought was so upsetting to her that her eyes were suddenly full of tears, completely blurring her vision. The crowd was beginning to disperse, and people were bumping into her, pushing her first in one direction and then the next. She was so upset and overwhelmed that before she realized it, she was on a strange part of the beach, with no idea which direction she had gone or how to get back. She fantasized about Paul swooping in to rescue her and holding her safely in his big, strong arms.

Stop being a stupid baby. She scolded herself. She wiped her eyes, trying to pull herself together. She had to formulate a plan, and for that, she had to sit and think. To calm herself down. She found a place in the sand to sit for a minute and closed her eyes, doing some deep breathing exercises that she had learned her freshman year. Any time she was feeling overwhelmed or stressed out she would practice this deep breathing and it made everything just a little bit easier to handle. Finally, after a few minutes, she felt clear-headed enough to figure out a solution to her problem. She started by asking random passersby if they knew which direction the tent was, but none of them knew what she was talking about. Instead, she started asking about the surfing demo, but even that took several tries before someone could point her in the right direction. She trudged through the sand, her cute sandals now cutting into her feet with every step. All she really wanted to do was to curl up somewhere dark and quiet and go to sleep, but she kept going, telling herself again that now was not the time to be a big pouty baby. There would be time for that later. She giggled at her own unfunny joke, despite her dire circumstances, and that made her feel a little better. She thought that she was starting to recognize her surroundings. Again, she felt a small ray of hope. Just as she was starting to feel like she might be ok again, the strap on her sandals broke, and she fell face-first into the sand. She heard a couple of snickers from the people around her, but one kind soul reached down to help her up.

"Oh dear," said the lady, who looked like a kindly grandmother. "You seem to have bumped your nose there. Here, have a tissue." The elderly lady fished in her bag for a crumpled up napkin, which Hannah took gratefully. The lady patted her hand sympathetically and waddled off. As Hannah dabbed at her nose, she saw that there was indeed blood on the tissue. At the sight of it, her knees grew weak, and she got very dizzy. She could feel herself sinking back down into the sand, a bit more gradually this time, hitting the sand with her knees first before everything went black.

***

When she woke up, Paul was kneeling over her, his handsome face scrunched up with concern. She had a disoriented moment where she wondered why he was in her bedroom. Then she remembered they were at the beach. She had been trying to find him, lost and upset. Then she remembered seeing the blood and fainting. Her head was aching, and she felt like an idiot lying in the sand like that. Frantically, she pulled her skirt down, praying that no one had seen her diaper as she lay sprawled out and unconscious. As she tried to sit up, however, a pair of strong hands was gently pushing her back down.

"Oh no you don't," said Paul. "You don't move a muscle until the EMTs can take a look at you." She groaned and covered her face in humiliation.

"No, please tell me you didn't call an ambulance. I only fainted, I'm fine."

"I called an ambulance and the cops," he replied. "When I tried to Facetime you, some guy answered and tried to extort money from me in exchange for your phone back. I figured that you must have been mugged or something, and I've been looking for you ever since. How long have you been lying out here like this?"

"I'm not sure, exactly. After I got mugged, I got lost. Then, my sandal broke, and my nose was bleeding, and I've never been good with blood." She trailed off, not wanting to cry in front of Paul.

"There, there little one," said Paul. "Don't cry. It's all my fault. I never should have left you alone like that. It will never happen again, I promise. I never dreamed that something like this could happen, can you ever forgive me?"

"Forgive you? What are you talking about? This wasn't your fault."

"Oh yes, it was," said Paul grimly. "I wasn't there to protect you. I didn't even leave you with a security guard. I should have known better."

"Paul,' she sighed, dreading telling him this next part. "I don't think you understand. They got your keys." Paul only laughed and shook his head at that, making Hannah squint at him in confusion.

"Good, that will only make it easier for the cops to find him. I always put a tracker in my key fobs because I lose them so frequently. Unless he's smart and ditches the fob. But don't you worry, I'll get your credit cards and I.D.s back from that guy, one way or another. You just leave it all up to me." She had no idea what to say in response to his unfaltering sweetness, but she was relieved of that burden when two EMTs pushed their way through the small crowd that had formed around them. They checked her out briefly, looking at her nose and pupils in particular. Eventually, they declared her to be in good health, saying that she was fine for now but that she should take it easy over the next couple of days. Once the EMTs were gone, Paul finally let her sit up. Now that it seemed that the show was over, the small crowd began to shuffle off as well.

"We need to get you off to bed right away," said Paul. He helped her up, handling her as delicately as possible as though she were made of glass. It was definitely touching but also a little embarrassing. As she put her arm through his to stabilize herself, she noticed that he had her broken sandal in his hand, and she almost started crying again, this time from gratitude.

"I really can't thank you enough. I honestly don't know what I'd do without you."

"That's enough of that, now," Paul said gently. "There is no point wondering what you'd do without me because you won't ever be without me again. Not if I have anything to say about it." She felt a flutter in her heart when he said that, feeling like the luckiest girl in the world to have him in her life. He had already done so much for her, made her feel so special. She leaned into Paul's warmth, taking comfort in his strength. He helped her get into the car and gave her back her broken sandal, but upon closer inspection, it didn't look salvageable. That's what happened when you bought cheap sandals, she supposed. Hannah gave him directions to her house, and they arrived there shortly. Once inside, he insisted that she sit down on the couch as he brought her blankets, books, and a cup of tea. Paul even threatened to make her some soup, but she declined, saying that she just wanted to rest for a while. Once she got him to settle, it actually turned out to be a lovely evening despite all the chaos from earlier. She changed out of the uncomfortable dress and put on some cute but comfy loungewear. The police called Paul to report that they had found the key fob ditched along with her purse and most of her IDs. She would have to cancel her credit cards, which were still missing and get a new phone, but at least she wouldn't have to go to the DMV.

Hannah would take the victory, even if it was a

small one. They streamed some movies and opened a bottle of wine to celebrate. He graciously let Hannah pick out her favorite movies. As they watched Dirty Dancing, Hannah snuck looks at her handsome guest when he wasn't looking, reflecting on what Paul had said earlier about how she would never have to be without him again. Now, she wondered what exactly he meant by that. She didn't want to get her hopes up, but she felt safe being cautiously optimistic as he snuggled in close to her. As they made their way through the first bottle of wine and then opened the second, she couldn't stop thinking about how he had looked out there on the waves, so graceful and assured of himself. He was a magnificent athlete, something that she was sure the result of many hours of practice. That sort of dedication was a very attractive quality to her. She couldn't help but wonder if that kind of stamina extended to the bedroom as well. As the credits began to roll on the movie, she noticed Paul looking at her with a very serious expression on his face.

"Can I ask you a question," he asked. She was almost sure that she detected a hint of nervousness in his voice, something she had never heard from him before. He usually seemed so confident.

"Of course you can," she said.

"I couldn't help but noticing that when you were lying in the sand earlier today, well, I could see your diaper." Her heart sank as she realized that her worst fears had come true. He knew her secret.

"I don't want to pressure you or anything," he continued. "You can tell me to mind my own business if you want. I was just kind of curious." She took a deep breath and decided that she didn't want to hide who she was anymore. He may not like it, but now that he knew, it almost felt like a relief.

"I just like wearing diapers sometimes. I know it's a little weird, but it makes me happy. It's like it calms me down or something." As the words came out, she felt her face get hot, and she looked down at her lap, avoiding his gaze. When she did peek up at him to gauge his reaction, she was surprised to see that he was grinning.

"You're a little. I was hoping that you were."

"You were?!" She had never heard anyone else speak of littles outside of the internet, and she'd always assumed that the odds were way too low ever to meet anyone in real life who shared her preferences.

"I was," he nodded. "You see, I'm a Daddy Dom, so I was secretly wishing that you were the little I've been looking for, I was just too nervous to say anything. I've had many a girl end our association after I've confessed that little tidbit."

"I've never told anyone," she said quietly. "I've always been afraid that they'd have exactly that reaction. You're so brave for telling them the truth. I'm sorry that they reacted that way."

"You're the brave one," he said. "I was too nervous to tell you, but now I don't have too." They beamed at one another, and Hannah felt a rush of joy at his praise. The joy was quickly replaced with a nervous awkwardness. Now that they knew that had that in common, where did that leave them? It might not mean anything. She tried to remind herself. It all just seemed too good to be true.

"Do you want to put another movie on, or are you ready to call it a night?" asked Paul. As he looked at her hopefully, she put those thoughts out of her mind. While she didn't want to get her hopes up, she also wanted to remain open to the possibilities.

"Yeah, I'm up for another. Let's watch Tootsie!" she said enthusiastically.

"Tootsie it is, then," said Paul and started the movie. As they settled back onto the couch, he took her hand in his. She looked at him in surprise, but he only smiled at her. It felt so warm and safe to be snuggled up so close to him on the couch, so right having his hands on her. Some part of her brain wanted to define what was happening, but she did her best not to listen to that part of herself and just enjoyed the moment. Paul poured her another glass of wine, handing it to her with a squeeze of her hand. She sipped it happily and passed it back to him, the two of them sharing one cup. Once the glass was empty, they snuggled together on the couch, a tangle of limbs and warm bodies. She closed her eyes, savoring the moment. It was both arousing and calming at the same time, and she wanted the evening to last forever.

Chapter 6

They must have fallen asleep like that because when Hannah awoke again, it was light outside. Paul was still asleep, and she was trapped under him, with Paul's head on her chest and his arms wrapped tightly around her waist. As much as she was loathe to break the moment, she really had to use the bathroom. Despite her best efforts to disentangle herself without waking him, Paul began to stir.

"Mmm, mornin' beautiful," he muttered as he opened his eyes blearily. "I didn't realize that we slept here." He rubbed his neck as if the night on the couch had left him feeling worse for wear.

"I guess it's a good thing," he said, stretching his arms. "Otherwise, you'd have no way of getting to work today. What time do you have to be in today?"

"Oh, not for a few more hours. We don't open until the afternoon."

"Great!" said Paul. "We have enough time for me to make waffles."

"You cook?" she asked, somewhat taken aback. This man was full of constant surprises. "That's so funny. I love to cook too. Come on. I'll show you where everything is." She gave him a brief tour of the kitchen before excusing herself to the lady's room. When she got back, Paul was in full chef mode. He had even dug out some chocolate chips from the cabinet and mixed them into the batter. He insisted that she sit down at the table and not lift a finger while he put on a pot of coffee. She sat and watched indulgently as he got breakfast ready. If she had a million wishes, she didn't think she could have ended up with a more perfect guy.

"So, where were you going to take me yesterday?" she asked.

"No spoilers," said Paul. "I'm still taking you. What time do you get off today?"

"Not that late, around six, usually. Sometimes I'll get lucky, and there won't be anyone signed up for that last tour, but things are just starting to get busy for the summer, so that probably won't happen."

"Well, leave your bathing suit on when you get off," said Paul. "And that's the only hint you get." She grinned and sipped her coffee coyly.

"Alright, then. I'm looking forward to it," she said.

***

He dropped her off after a delicious breakfast. The day at work seemed to drag on, doubly so because it was Claire's day off, and she couldn't even gossip about the events that her so giddy. She could only watch the clock anxiously and wonder about the surprise they would have for her at the end of her shift. All day, the only thing she could think about was how she had finally found a real-life Daddy. And what's more, she really liked him. Thoughts of diaper changes and spankings danced in her head. She wouldn't have to hide who she was around him. Just that simple fact alone had her practically walking on air. Finally, it was time to clock out. Paul was already waiting for her in his car when she came outside. No matter how she pleaded or begged, he still would not tell her where they were going.

"You're just going to have to live with the suspense," he teased. She pretended to pout, but Paul put his hand on her knee, and she couldn't suppress her grin. At that moment, she felt so happy, with the wind in her hair and the best companion that anyone could ask for. They drove out of the city and out past the suburbs. Soon they were in a part of the island that Hannah had never been to before. It was very rural, and they only passed houses and gas stations. Eventually, they turned down a driveway and came to a gate. Paul punched in a code on the keypad, and they were in. The driveway ended onto a private beach. It was stunningly beautiful. The sand was the purest she had ever seen, almost white as the evening sun bounced off it. The water was a stunning blue-green, clear, and pure. There was not a living soul around them. They had the whole place to themselves. Hannah had never felt so free.

"This is amazing!" she said, looking around in wonder. She shed her shorts and t-shirt, eager to get into the water right away.

"I thought that you of all people would appreciate this," he said, taking her hand and leading her toward the shoreline. She kicked off her flip flops, letting the cool sand kiss her bare feet. The two of them ran into the surf, letting the waves break over their bodies. They dove under and swam far from the shore before finally coming up for air. They laughed as they surfaced, exhilarated by one another, and their shared love of the sea.

"You're a very strong swimmer," said Paul. She noticed that he was still gripping her hand. He suddenly dropped her hand, opting instead to wrap one arm around her waist, pulling her close to him. Paul was nearly facing her, close enough that he could kiss her, a thought that left Hannah breathless. He placed a small soft kiss on the curve of her neck. The brush of his lips sent a jolt of electricity all through her. She gasped slightly as Paul's arms tightened around her waist, and he placed a kiss on the other side of her neck as well. She was flooded with so many sensations and emotions that she felt absolutely overwhelmed. Paul continued his soft kisses on her neck as he began to run his hands over her waist and hips. A wave of arousal, stronger than any she had ever experienced before, took her over as he kissed and caressed her body. She closed her eyes to savor the sensations. He claimed her lips with his, salty, and passionate, and she ran her fingers through his hair. She was so adrift in the pleasure that she would have certainly slipped below the surface if she didn't have a strong man holding her afloat. His tongue was suddenly pushing into her mouth with an eagerness to taste her. She moaned into his open mouth and grabbed at his shoulders to bring him closer. She could feel his erection pressing against her, igniting her desire further.

"Let's go back ashore," she murmured, wanting to be on solid ground so that she could explore him the same way he was exploring her. He took her hands and they both dove under the waves again, gliding under the water back toward the shore. Once their feet could touch the bottom, he was all over again, only this time, her hands were free to roam over his firm, muscled bodies, as she had been longing to do for days. The waves crashed over them as they explored one another with lips, tongues, and hands. He pulled aside her bathing suit, delving his fingers into her aching center, seeking out her most sensitive spot. As he pleasured her, he pulled her straps down to release her ample breasts so that he could claim her nipples with his mouth, kissing and licking them so lovingly. She let herself go completely, leaning her head back as her moans echoed down the empty beach. She could feel the pleasure building, working toward a crescendo. Her hands reached out blindly, looking for something to grab or hold onto. Paul took her hands in his, holding them as he continued to kiss her neck and breasts. His fingers between her legs felt like pure heaven, and as much as she wanted to make this perfect moment last, she couldn't hold back anymore. As the ecstasy broke over her, she cried out and gripped Paul's hand as her body shook. As she came back to herself, sated and content, she wanted to return the pleasure that she had just received. She released Paul's hands and sought out the hardness within his swim trunks. He gave a shuddering gasp as she slipped her hand down past the elastic and gripped him firmly. She stroked him lovingly as their tongues dancing together. Paul quickly gave in to his release. He grabbed her face, kissing her deeply and passionately as she swallowed his moans. He didn't let her come up for air until the last shudder had left his body and his breath began to slow.

He's so perfect. She thought as they clung to each other in the surf and sand. After a few minutes, they made their way slowly further away from the shoreline, collapsing in a heap on the sand, still breathless and giddy. They snuggled close together, his arms encircling her in a tight hug. As she gazed up at the stars that were just barely starting to become visible, she felt like thanking them. They lay like that for so long, reluctant to move lest it would break the magic spell of their happiness, that it was fully dark by the time they began to stir. Reluctantly, they got up, brushing the sand from their bodies and hair. On the way back into town, Hannah stared dreamily out of the window before closing her eyes with a smile on her face and the wind in her hair.

Chapter 7

They went back to Paul's so that she would be able to pick up his other car. He had picked up another fob and retrieved it from the beach while she was at work. The latest update on hers was that the part was in; it was just a matter of waiting for the labor to be finished. When she asked about the expense, he only waved away the question.

"Don't worry about it," Paul said, winking at her. "I already told you, you don't pay for anything when you're with me." He pressed the keys into her hand and kissed her on her forehead. She wanted to protest that it was too much, too extravagant, but then she thought about how many shifts at the marina it would take to pay off such a high mechanic bill and about the student loan payments that she was going to have to start paying soon. And that would be on top of the credit card payments she already struggled to keep up with. If she didn't get a job in her field soon, there would be no way for her to keep up with all of that.

"Well, if you're sure," she said, an edge of uncertainty in her voice.

"Never been surer of anything," said Paul, taking her hand reassuringly. "He's going to cut me a deal since we're friends, and what little bit of cash it will cost will be my graduation present to you." She smiled at that, suddenly feeling much better.

"I suppose I do deserve a graduation present, don't I?" she said playfully, giving him a kiss on the cheek. "Well, I'd better get back home. It's been a really lovely evening, thank you."

"You don't want to stay?" he asked, placing a gentle kiss on the nape of her neck like a little added incentive. "I promise not to keep you up too late." As he pressed his body against hers, Hannah had a suspicion that they would be up very late indeed but found that she didn't mind one bit. He ran his fingertips up and down her back as he kissed and nuzzled her neck and she felt herself turn to putty in his hands. Feeling emboldened, she suddenly grabbed him by his firm buttocks and pulled him closer so that his erection was pressing against her. Her body cried out with a burning need to have him inside of her. He groaned at the intimate contact, and his hot breath against her neck made her ache for him all the more.

"Oh Daddy," she whispered on instinct. At the sound of it, Paul suddenly became fierce, grabbing her by the face to pull her in for a passionate, demanding kiss while at the same time pushing her against the door of his home so that she was trapped between him and the unyielding wood door. She had dreamed for so long of being handled exactly in such a manner but had never experienced it until now. It was everything she had imagined it would be as she felt a clenching heat at her core. As he growled into her mouth, biting her lip and pressing his hard cock against her, she melted into him, wanting him to possess her completely. He began fumbling with the lock as they kissed, not wanting to tear himself away from her even for a second. As he flung the door open, she wrapped her arms around his neck. He hoisted her by the ass, lifting her into his arms, and she wrapped her legs around him as well. He kicked the door closed and began carrying her upstairs, exploring her mouth with his tongue the entire way. He put her down again as they entered his bedroom. Paul got on the bed and looked at her up and down, his eyes hungrily taking in her every feature.

"Strip," said Paul, his voice suddenly taking on an authoritativeness that her body responded to instantly. "I want to see my baby girl." She smiled bashfully, taking off the t-shirt she had on over her bathing suit slowly as his eyes tracked her every movement. Paul began to undo his belt, never taking his eyes off of her as he did so. She slid off her shorts, letting them fall to the floor, leaving her only in her bathing suit. It wasn't the sexiest of lingerie, admittedly, but you would never know that based on the way Paul was looking at her.

"You're so beautiful, little one," Paul said, making her blush deeply. No one had ever looked at her so intensely before, and it filled her with a hungry desire. She ran her hands slowly over her stomach before peeling the top of her suit down. Judging from the sharp inhale from Paul, he liked what he saw.

"Fuck, your tits are so perfect," Paul growled, his voice now thick and velvety with lust. "Everything about you is absolutely perfect." Knowing that she was having such an effect as he watched her, that he was so aroused by her was such an aphrodisiac.

"Now take the rest of it off, right now," he commanded. Hannah gasped as her core clenched with desire, and she hurriedly obeyed, eager to give him whatever he asked for. She was thoroughly intoxicated by his domination over her. Her pussy was dripping wet already, even though he had barely touched her. As she peeled the suit the rest of the way down and proudly displayed herself for him, she heard Paul growl "good girl" and she was filled with glowing pride.

"You're mine now, princess," Paul's voice was hypnotic, commanding. "Every part of you, every inch of you now belongs to me. Do you understand me?"

"Yes." Hannah felt breathless, standing before him, vulnerable and completely naked. Her body yearned for him more powerfully than she ever thought was possible. The raw hunger on his face made her tremble, longing to be consumed by him.

"Say it," said Paul gruffly, his usually sweet voice turned rough with lust. Her body ached for them, and she felt like she was completely under their spell.

"I am yours, every inch of me belongs to you." She could feel herself growing even more excited as she said the words, feeling the weight of what she was promising. Paul was beginning to rub himself over his pants, making the outline of his erection more visible. Hannah licked her lips, unable to take her eyes off of it.

"That's right. Fuck, you are so perfect. Come here right now." She joined him on the bed, kneeling before him. His hands were all over her, caressing her adoringly yet urgently. She let her eyes close as his touches grew bolder, exploring the curve of her hips, her generous breasts, and the heat between her legs. Passionate energy radiated from him, leaving her feeling breathless. He pulled her down onto the bed, and she reclined against the pillows as he began to cover her naked flesh with kisses. She returned his caresses, kissing him with all of the fiery need that she felt inside. The orgasm he had given her earlier had did very little to sate her hunger for him. As Paul took her nipple in his mouth, she moaned loudly, and it was as if she were galvanized by him. Her electric desire made her impatient, and she took his hand, guiding it to the very center of her desire. His mouth trailed behind his hand, making her shiver with delight. He found her clit with his soft tongue as he slipped his finger inside of her. The pleasure was so intense that she could only moan and writhe on the bed as Paul pleasured her. His fingers and tongue were so skillful that she knew it wouldn't be long before she climaxed again. She gripped Paul's silky hair, holding on for dear life as the pleasure built. As much as she longed to make it last, the ecstasy was too much, and she could hold back no longer. Her thighs trembled as she peaked, and he lapped at her faster, wanting to draw every ounce of pleasure from her that he could. She collapsed back against the pillows, her breath ragged and her heart racing. He made a soft noise of pleasure and wrapped himself around her, cocooning her as her breathing slowly returned to normal. It wasn't long before she was reaching out for him with a barely sated hunger. Even through his pants, she could feel his desire for her, and she knew that he too needed much more than what they had shared at the beach. She began fumbling with his zipper, making little progress before he became impatient and swatted her hands away. She waited eagerly as he shed all of his clothes, tossing them onto the floor in a heap. He lay on his back next to her, and she grasped his cock eagerly. He looked so sexy, sprawled out before her, naked and eager for her. She took a moment to enjoy his naked form, toned and smooth before taking him into her mouth, delighting in the way he threw his head back and moaned with abandon as she swallowed his member. She closed her eyes as she tongued the underside of the tip, savoring the taste of him. He put his hand under chin, lifting her face slightly.

"Look at me," he said. She opened her eyes again to see him staring down at her with an intensity she had never seen before. His breath quickened, and he stroked her cheek, gazing down at her with open adoration. Keeping her eyes locked on his, she began to work his shaft further and further down her throat, getting a thrill from the look of agonized pleasure on his face. That look emboldened her, made her begin to pick up her pace with enthusiasm, loving the effect she was clearly having on him. As she pleasured Paul with her mouth, but he began to grow dissatisfied with that, shifting his position on the bed so that he was behind her. She could feel his hardness pressing against her folds, but he didn't penetrate her. Instead teased her labia and clit with the tip of his cock. She moaned and squirmed against him, his teasing reigniting the fire inside of her. Her body sought out what it needed, inching him closer and closer to her entrance, desperate to have him inside of her. Hannah felt almost hypnotized, her body tingled with desire, and she longed for Paul to fill her aching pussy. He seemed to be enjoying teasing her, however, rubbing himself against her but never plunging in as she desperately wanted him to.

"What's the matter?" Paul whispered. "Do you want me to fuck you, little one?" She whimpered and nodded. The sensation of his rigid member against her aching sex was driving her wild and she needed satisfaction.

"I'll be happy to oblige you," he teased and then leaned in, growling into her ear. "But you'll have to ask for it." She shivered as he ran the tip of his cock over her clit, rubbing it in slow circles over her swollen nub, breaking down the very last of her inhibitions. Somewhat reluctantly, she took Paul out of her mouth long enough to ask for what she desperately needed.

"Oh Daddy, please fuck me, I need you so bad!" Some part of herself was surprised to hear that kind of language coming out of her mouth, but mostly it only made her feel strangely liberated to give voice to her desires. He plunged into her finally, groaning with satisfaction as he buried himself inside of her to the hilt. Her entire body felt alive as he stretched her open, taking her hard and fast.

"Is that what you wanted, princess?" he moaned into her ear.

"Yes, oh yes," she said enthusiastically. She rocked back to meet his every thrust, lost in a sea of lust and the early blossoming of love. As his thick cock split her open again and again, she could feel another climax building. She reached down to rub her clit, the extra layer of pleasure sending her over the edge. Her whole body quivered as her intense orgasm took her over.

"Good girl," she heard Paul whisper as she moaned wildly around his cock. "You're so tight around my cock. You're going to make me cum, little one!" As Hannah's quaking orgasm began to recede, his thrusts quickened. She could feel his manhood grow even harder inside of her, throbbing on the edge of release. His rhythm suddenly faltered, and his body went rigid. His cock throbbed and twitched inside of her as he filled her up with his seed. Hannah moaned wildly, intoxicated by the sensation. With one final shudder, he collapsed against her and buried his face in her neck.

"Good girl," he whispered shakily, patting the back of her head gently. With a happy grin, she wrapped her arms around him, cradling him. Lying beneath him like that, Hannah felt the happiest she had ever been. His hands glided lovingly over her skin, both soothing and arousing her and Paul kissed her deeply on the lips.

"You are mine now. All mine." She felt her heart melt open in a way it never had before, leaving her feeling raw and vulnerable. Every cell in her body knew it was true, knew that this man was her future.

"All yours," she echoed, her voice hazy with a dreamy contentment. They clung to each other, and she had never felt so safe, so contented. She held him close, kissed his sweaty forehead, and thought about how she would love to stay like that forever.

Chapter 8

Paul had other ideas, however, and his tender caresses grew heated once more. To her surprise, she found that his hunger fueled her own and she found herself already craving more of him. *Who knew I was such a little minx?* It was Paul who brought that out in her, she realized. He buried his face in her breasts, frantically kissing, licking, and sucking her tender flesh. He held her tightly against him as he devoured her, grinding her already wet pussy against him, still slick with their combined juices. Her happy sighs turned to moans as he twisted her body so that he could smack her ass, lightly at first, but then with increasing intensity.

"Do you like it when Daddy spanks you, little one?" he murmured against her nipple. She moaned and squirmed against him, wanting him to continue.

"Yes, Daddy. Spank my ass, please." He grinned up at her and her stomach fluttered with excitement.

"I was hoping you would say that Princess." She gasped in surprise as he pushed her face down onto the bed so that she was on all fours. He rubbed her backside lovingly for a moment, and the anticipation of what would come next made her whine and squirm. Knowing that she was about to get the spanking she had longed for for so long made her go from wet to dripping almost instantly. He slapped her ass forcefully, even harder than he had before. She yelped and jerked at the sharp pain, gritting her teeth as she fought to take it like a good girl. As much as it hurt, it also made her pussy ache. He followed it up with two more swift, sharp blows, making her yelp again. He chuckled at her response and caressed her flesh tenderly with his fingertips.

"What do you think of that, kitten? Do you still like it when Daddy spanks you? Should I keep going?" Her hips automatically thrust back, her buttocks seeking more of the invigorating combination of pleasure and pain. She nodded her head and whimpered, wordlessly asking for more.

"Use your words, kitten," he said sternly, popping her already tender buttcheeks playfully. Even that felt good, even though she craved the harder blows.

"Yes, Daddy," she gasped, overwhelmed by her burning desire. "Please, spank me more!" She hid her face in the pillows of the bed as he delivered blow after blow to her meaty buttocks. She squealed and squirmed as he increased the intensity, each blow landing harder than the last, but she made no move to stop him. Indeed, every blow brought closer to a kind of frenzy, her whole body singing with desire. Suddenly, the onslaught ceased, and he once again stroked her tender flesh, admiring his work. She peeked at him over her shoulder, his face was flushed, and he was breathing heavily, his eyes fixated on her bottom.

"Oh, sweetie, your little bum is so pink," he

said quietly. His fingers on her backside felt so good, and once again, her hips rose, giving him access to all of her. He took the hint and began to lightly trace her cleft, tracing all the way down to the very center of her desire. He gently exploring her folds, holding her gaze with his own as he touched her. The way he stared into her eyes as if he could see her very soul made her heart flutter.

"You're so wet, you dirty little thing. I'm going to have so much fun with you." He twirled his fingertips around her clit, making her eyes roll back in her head. She was so overwhelmed with the sensation that she could neither squeal nor moan, only grip the pillows and writhe on the bed. Just as she thought that it couldn't get more intense, he once again brought his open hand down on her tender rear end. She cried out as she lost all sense of control, surrendering completely to his mastery over her body. He noted her reaction and continued spanking her as he fingered her until she was a gasping, dripping mess.

"You're not about to cum, are you princess?" He smacked her twice in a row, painful smacks that made her jump and gasp, getting ever closer to a powerful orgasm. "Remember, you're mine now. That means you don't cum until I give you permission. Is that understood?"

"Yes, Daddy," she gasped. Her entire body aching at his words. It was so erotic, the thought of him having such absolute control over her body and mind like that, giving or denying pleasure at his whim. He plunged a finger into her aching entrance, bringing her closer to a screaming climax. It took all of her willpower to hold back as he pumped his finger in and out of her, rubbing her most sensitive spot with every stroke. How did he expect her to control herself when he did things like that to her?

"Please, Daddy," she whined. "Please, it feels so good. I want to cum so bad." He didn't seem convinced and spanked her hard, sending sparks of pain and ecstasy all through her. Her tender bottom was beginning to feel raw and bruised, and her body was screaming for release.

"I think you can do better than that, little one."

"Please, Daddy. It feels so good when you spank me and fuck my slutty little pussy. Please, can I cum Daddy, can I?" After all those times she had chastised Claire for using crass language, she couldn't believe that such filth came so easily from her mouth. She found that she didn't care, the dirty words only bringing her closer to the edge. He seemed to love torturing her, sliding a second finger into her, stretching her out. She kicked her legs and squealed, feeling incredibly full and closer than ever to coming without permission. If he didn't give her release soon, she felt she would lose her mind.

"Daddy, please, I can't take it. Please let me cum!"

"Ok, princess, you've been a good girl. You can come for Daddy." He smacked her ass as he pumped his fingers into her, sending Hannah over the edge. Her entire body shook as fingers drove into her relentlessly, demanding more and more with every thrust.

"That's it, kitten. Let it all out. Daddy knows how to take care of this slutty little pussy. There's a good girl." He did not let up until she collapsed against the mattress, panting and utterly spent. He rubbed her butt and back tenderly as she lay there, too exhausted to move. It was as if her entire body had turned to jelly. She couldn't remember ever having cum so hard. She gave a shaky sigh as he removed his fingers and brought them to his mouth, licking them with a satisfied moan. He was so naughty and so sexy. Paul gripped her tender buttocks, delighting in the way it made her whimper and squirm. She could feel his manhood pressing against her dripping pussy, ready to claim her. He didn't seem to be in any particular hurry, however, and took his time kissing her back. She began to moan and writhe against him, her body already on fire again, yearning for more despite the powerful orgasm she'd had just moments before. He wrapped his strong arms around her and held her tightly as he kissed and bit her neck. She thrust her hips up, moaning softly. She felt helpless pinned underneath him like that, and that helplessness was exhilarating.

"Are you already hungry for more, my darling?" he teased playfully as she whined, overwhelmed by her aching need. He moved his hand down to grab the bruised flesh of her buttocks again, digging his fingers into the tender skin as he pulled her closer against his throbbing member. She opened her legs wider as the tip of his cock brushed her labia. He was so close to being inside her, it would take just a tiny little thrust, and she could ease this burning desire within. She felt him run his thumb over her rear entrance and shuddered, totally unprepared for the electric jolt it sent throughout her body.

"What are you doing?" she gasped.

"Do you want me to stop, baby?" he purred.

"No," she shivered, finding that she very much wanted him to keep going. "I like that. It feels really nice." She had never been stimulated there before, had never even given it much thought, but as Paul ran circles around her rear entrance, it made her pussy react strongly. He dipped his thumb into her slick juices giving his thumb more slip as he slowly began to sink it in, moving gradually to allow her body time to adjust to the new intrusion. After a moment, he began to work it in and out of her, and she squealed and squirmed with delight.

"Oh, Daddy," she cried out, too lost in lust to be bashful any longer. "Daddy, please fuck my ass." Just as she was beginning to think that she might climax again just from his thumb in her rear, Paul pulled it out of her ass and replaced it with the tip of his member. Slowly, he began to push himself into her, stretching out her rear end with his thick cock. As he began to fill her, Hannah screamed and thrashed underneath him. It felt more amazing than anything she had ever experienced before. As he inched his way in, she was fascinated by delicious combination of pain and pleasure, and she only wanted more and more. He was slick with her juices and slid in easily yet was careful not to go too quickly lest he hurt her. He pushed himself past the rim, her tight ass hugging the tip of his cock. She thrust her hips back, wanting to take more of him inside of her. He let her control the pace, letting her fuck herself deeper and deeper with his cock. She thrust herself all the way back, taking him completely inside her body. Paul took that as a green light and began to pound into her. She surrendered herself to him and held on as he unleashed his passion for her, thrusting into her hard and fast. He gripped her hips, pulling her back so that he could bury himself in her back passage. Hannah could feel her orgasm building, knew it would be long before it came crashing over her and she would be powerless to stop it. Before she could even form a thought, she was already coming again. Her eyes rolled back, and she cried out, louder than ever before, coming totally undone as he brought her to greater heights of pleasure than she ever knew was possible.

"Oh, fuck. You're so tight. Am I the first one

to fuck your ass?"

"Yes, Daddy," she moaned. "Fuck my virgin ass, please!" It seemed that she couldn't take any more pleasure as he thrust into her over and over. They both moaned and writhed together, lost in a bliss that felt so good and so right that she also didn't ever want it to be over. Paul went over the edge once more, biting down on her shoulder as he stiffened and filled her with his seed again. She shivered with delight at the feeling of being so full of his warm semen and moaned with satisfaction as he collapsed into a sweaty, breathless heap on top of her. Neither of them could speak; they could only hold each other closely. Sated at last, they basked in their contentment. She was sure that she was the luckiest woman alive and that she had the most wonderful man on the planet right here with her.

Chapter 9

"Would you like me to put you in a diaper?" he asked. Hannah had been very close to falling asleep, but the suggestion made her sit straight up. The thought of having yet another fantasy fulfilled this evening made her heart pound. He really was her dream come to life.

"Yes, Daddy, I would like that very much." His face lit up, and he went into his closet, rummaging around until he came back with a pack of diapers.

"I've been saving these," he said. "Hoping to have the opportunity to use them one day."

"You've never diapered anyone before?" she asked.

"No," he shook his head. "This will be my first time." She grinned at that, suddenly feeling very proud to be his first. It also put her more at ease, knowing that she wasn't the only one experiencing all of this for the first time. He took the diaper out of the package and gently spread her knees open with his hands.

"Hips up, little one," he said and slid the diaper underneath her. He took a moment to admire her naked form before fastening the diaper closed. "You're so beautiful, princess. Do you ever wet your diaper?"

"I do," she admitted shyly. "Especially at night."

"Good girl," he grinned, patting the front of her diaper approvingly. "In that case, I expect to see a very full diaper in the morning, is that understood?"

"Yes, Daddy," she said, returning her grin. It felt like such a relief to not only be open about her lifestyle around him but to share it with him as well. It was so liberating to know that he not only tolerated it, he craved it as much as she did. He rejoined her on the bed and wrapped her in his arms once again. She burrowed her face into his chest, savoring his masculine scent.

"Sorry that I don't have any stuffies or anything else that a little might enjoy. I'll go pick up some things tomorrow while you're out."

"That's ok, Daddy. You can be my stuffie tonight," she said, stifling a yawn. He chuckled and kissed her forehead.

"Sounds like it's bedtime for you, little one. Get a good night's sleep."

"You too, Daddy." He held her tightly as she drifted off to sleep with a happy smile on her face.

***

When she awoke, Paul was still asleep. The pressure on her bladder told her that she had not yet wet herself as she had promised. She released her urine into the diaper, soaking it thoroughly. As the warm liquid soaked into the absorbent fabric, she thought her new Daddy would be very pleased with her, and it filled her with pride. She took a moment to admire his handsome face as he slept.

It felt so nice to finally have a Daddy that she could call her very own. She had dreamed of this for so long, and it was finally here. Some part of her still felt like this was all just a wonderful dream. At last, Paul began to stir. She placed a gentle kiss on his cheek, and his eyes fluttered open.

"Good morning, princess," he whispered. "Did you sleep well?"

"Yes, Daddy. I need you to change me, please." He opened his eyes wider and smiled at her. He had such a lovely smile, she thought. Even lovelier when it was because of her.

"Oh, is that so? Let me see." He lifted the covers and peeked at her puffy, full diaper. With one hand, he reached down and patted the front approvingly. "Yes, you did a very good job, little one. Daddy is very proud of you." He peeled the covers off of her and fished around for some baby wipes. As he unfastened the tabs and pulled her diaper down, he took in a deep breath.

"Yes, that's what I was hoping to see. You did a very good job, princess."

"Thank you, Daddy," she said, blushing and glowing with pride at the same time. She lifted her hips so that he could slide the soiled diaper from beneath her. He bundled it up and tossed it in the trash. Taking a wipe from the pack, he lovingly cleaned her. The soft material felt so good against her pussy, and it felt even better to be so tenderly pampered.

"Would you like to take a shower with me, pumpkin?" he asked as he tossed the wipe away.

"Mmm, that sounds nice," she smiled. He took her by the hands and helped her onto her feet. He took a moment to wrap her tightly in his arms, their naked, warm bodies pressed against one another. Then, he took her by the hand and led her into the bathroom. After getting the water temperature just right, he pulled her under the stream with him. He washed her from head to toe, lovingly sudsing up every inch of her body and then rinsing her clean again. As he bathed her, his cock came to life, and Hannah wanted so badly to taste him. Paul caught her peeking and stroked his cock seductively as she watched.

"I know you want to suck my cock," he teased. "Isn't that right, my dirty little princess?" She watched, hypnotized, as he slowly stroked his member, never once taking his eyes off of her naked body. She could only nod, feeling dazed and speechless with lust. He laughed, clearly enjoying the mesmerizing effect he was having over her.

"Get on your knees," he growled, and she obeyed instantly, warm water cascading over her body as she knelt before him. She took his juicy member in her hands, a shiver of excitement going through her. She guided his throbbing cock to her lips, moaning with pleasure as she tasted him.

"I told you last night to look at me when you suck my cock," he barked, and she looked up to meet his gaze. "Good little slut. Keep your eyes on me. Remember who you belong to." His words set her on fire, and she began to bob her head up and down on his erection. She took more and more of him down her throat, her excitement, and eagerness to please him, lowering her inhibitions.

No matter how far down her throat she was able to take him, she still craved more, choking herself with his throbbing cock over and over.

"Slow down," he whispered. "I'm not done with you yet." He pulled her to her feet and pushed her face-first against the bathroom tile. He pulled her hands behind her, holding both of her wrists with one hand as he slapped her ass hard, sending a jolt of pain and pleasure through her that left her weak in the knees and blind with lust. Her ass was slightly bruised from the night before, and he took his time, adding a few more bruises until she was whimpering and squirming. He ran his hand lightly over her tender buttocks, growling with satisfaction.

"Oh baby, you look so perfect," he whispered. "Now you're marked by me, and you'll always have a reminder that you're my baby girl." She shivered. That feeling of belonging to him was so intoxicating, and her body cried out for him, wanting him to claim her yet again. He slid his finger inside her needy pussy first, and it felt so good that she saw stars. She moaned loudly, bucking her hips back.

"You like that, huh? Naughty little slut." He pulled his finger out, replacing it with the tip of his cock, and slowly began to push in. She hissed with satisfaction as he slowly eased himself in, stretching her open inch by inch. With a fierce growl, he rammed himself the rest of the way into her. She gasped and collapsed against the tile wall, letting herself get totally lost in the pleasure. He slammed into her harder and harder, and she could feel herself building to a climax.

"Oh fuck, Daddy. You're going to make me cum!" she cried out.

"You'd better not, little one. I want you to be desperate and horny for me all day long. I want this little cunt of yours to be so drippy and needy that you can't wait to get off work and rush over to be my little fuck-slave again." Again she wondered how he expected her not to cum all over his cock when he said deliciously nasty things like that to her. Suddenly, he gripped her hips harder, pulling her back against him. With his throbbing cock buried deep inside of her, he let out a roar and pumped her full of his hot cum. It was so hard not to cum with him, but she held herself back, eager to be a good girl for him. As he pulled out of her, she could only twitch and moan quietly. Even after being denied an orgasm, she felt more satisfied than she ever had before. Just knowing that she had pleased him made her happy, and she looked forward to a day of burning for more of him. She could feel his hot semen dripping out and shivered with delight at the sensation. It felt so good to be full of him, to know that she served him well. He put his hand under her chin, pulling her face to his for a gentle kiss. She bathed him in the same way that he had bathed her. Running her hands over sudsy muscles only made the ache between her legs more intense, but she found that she enjoyed the ache. As he had said earlier, it reminded her who she belonged to and that was the best feeling in the world.

Chapter 10

He dropped her off at work a few hours later. At first, she assumed she would take his spare car, but he said that he wanted to spend the extra time with her. As he drove her, he casually fondled her, stroking her pussy and tweaking her nipples so that she was burning with desire for him with no possible source of relief. She whined that it wasn't fair, but secretly she hoped that he wouldn't stop. It was as cruel as it was hot. After he dropped her off with a deep passionate kiss, she filled in Claire on all the developments that had happened since she last saw her. As she recapped the surfing competition, their night on the couch together, and their trip to the private beach, Claire hung onto her every word.

"Wait, wait. So you're telling me that you two are together now?!" Hannah blushed, thinking to herself that Claire didn't even know the half of it. Together didn't even begin to describe what was happening between her and Paul.

"Yeah, I guess we are," she giggled, knowing that Claire would never really understand even if she did explain it.

"Ugh, you lucky bitch. Did you two do it yet?" Hannah wasn't used to sharing such intimate details, even with friends, but the deep blush that came over her face told Claire everything she needed to know. She jumped up and down, squealing and clapping. "Oh my god, it's about time you got some. How was it?"

"Um, it was - "Hannah was saved by the bell, or rather by her cell phone ringing. She held up a finger to Claire as she answered it.

"Tell me later," Claire mouthed and went outside to meet her group.

"Hello?"

"Hello, this Bob Chance with the Brighter Day Aquarium. "I got your information from Mr. Peterson. He was quite enthusiastic about your capabilities, and he is a difficult man to impress. We were hoping that you would be willing to come in for an interview." Hannah struggled not to whoop for joy and somehow managed to schedule a time to meet with Mr. Chance without squealing or babbling too much. As she hung up the phone, tears of joy and gratitude streamed down her face. He had never even mentioned that he'd put in a good word for her, and here she was with an interview for her dream job all lined up. If she thought she was going to be counting down the minutes until she got off work before, it was going to be sheer torture now. She couldn't wait to get back to Paul's to show him just how grateful she truly was.

"Come on, Hannah, your group is waiting," Mr. Williams poked his head into the breakroom, looking sweaty and annoyed. Hannah looked up at him in surprise and wiped a tear from her eye, and he quickly softened. "Oh hey, don't cry about it." Hannah shook her head and chuckled slightly, realizing that she probably looked a mess.

"It's not you, Mr. Williams. I just got some good news."

"Oh, well congratulations then, I guess. Tell you what, take a minute to pull yourself together. I'll tell them you're in the bathroom with a stomach ache or something." He was gone before she could point out that they might not want to be in the water with someone with a stomach ache. She shook her head with a smile as she went into the bathroom to splash water on her face before going out to give what would hopefully be one of her last dolphin tours.

***

Paul was already waiting for her in the parking lot, and she ran out to greet him with a huge smile on her face.

"Guess what," she gushed, too excited to even giving him a chance to guess. "I got a call from Mr. Chance today, and I have an interview with him in two days."

"That's fantastic news!" he exclaimed and wrapped her in a huge bear hug. "Looks like we have something to celebrate tonight. Other than finding each other that is." The last part, he whispered in her ear, and it sent a shiver of delight through her. She had been on a cloud of happiness and horniness all day, and now, with his body pressed against her, the heat that had been building all day suddenly overwhelmed her. He kissed her forehead and opened the car door for her. As he got into the driver's seat, he started the car but didn't put it into gear. He turned to her, a look of predatory hunger on his face.

"Have you been thinking about being my little fuck-slave all day like I told you to?" he asked, reaching over to put his hand over her crotch. She shuddered and groaned at his touch.

"Yes, Daddy," she whispered, her eyes fluttering closed.

"Show me," he demanded. "Pull down your shorts." She took a nervous look around before unbuttoning her shorts and sliding them down over her hips and onto the floorboard. He pushed aside her bathing suit bottom and dipped his finger between her moist folds. "Oh baby girl, you are so wet."

"I've been tingling for you all day," she sighed. He sat back with a smile and pulled his finger back. He snickered at the way she whimpered.

"Show Daddy again where the tingles are," he said with a wicked glint in his eyes. Again, she looked out of the window nervously.

"But what if someone sees?" she asked.

"Then they'll see a good little slut who does what she's told," he growled, totally unconcerned. "Show me right now." His eyes followed her every movement as she pulled her bathing suit farther to the side and parted her folds for him to see.

"Touch your clit." She put her finger on her sensitive spot as he watched her closely.

"Good girl. Now stroke it." She did as he said, twirling her finger around her swollen clit and moaning softly as it sent ripples of pleasure all through her body. Already, she felt ready to explode at a moment's notice.

"Like that, Daddy?" she asked, as eager to please him as she was to release her pent up desire.

"Slower, baby girl. I don't want you to cum just yet. You're so cute when you squirm and whine." She slowed her pace as he instructed, the slower pace amplifying every sensation, making her entire body ache for more.

"Yes, Daddy," she sighed, delighting yet again at the control he had over her body and her pleasure. "I'll be a good girl."

"I know you will. You're Daddy's good girl." He watched with silent fascination as she fingered herself and moaned softly.

"Stop," he said suddenly. She took my finger away but stuck out her bottom lip, which only made him grin wickedly. "So cute. You want to cum so badly don't you, my greedy little princess?"

"Yes, Daddy," she whined.

"Good girl, that's how Daddy likes you.

Now, put your finger inside that tight little pussy of yours." She sank her finger into her eager hole, seeking out the sweet spot under his watchful eye. As she found it, she sighed with pleasure and let her eyes roll back in her head.

"Does that feel good, pumpkin?" His voice was so thick with lust that it too added another layer to her pleasure.

"Yes, Daddy. That feels so good, thank you for letting me finger my greedy pussy."

"You're welcome, baby girl. Now, move it in and out slowly. And remember, no cumming yet." She moved her finger in and out of her aching pussy as slowly as she could. He looked absolutely ready to devour her, but he only watched her patiently, seemingly in no rush at all. "I know that greedy pussy is aching for more. Use two fingers." She swallowed and put a second finger inside, inching it in slowly. She could feel herself stretch open to accommodate it, and it felt so delicious that she let her head roll back and moaned loudly, no longer concerned about who might see or hear.

"See kitten? I know what that slutty little pussy of yours needs. Isn't that right?"

"Yes, Daddy knows," she said, knowing that it was true.

"Daddy knows about what?" he teased. She shivered, loving the way he made her say the dirtiest things.

"Daddy knows what my slutty little pussy needs," she gasped, her voice taking on a high pitched, pleading quality.

"Daddy?"

"Yes, baby girl?" He never took his eyes off her fingers as they went in and out of her dripping pussy.

"Can I cum? I need to cum. Pretty please?" She hoped that if she asked very nicely, he would grant her request, and she would finally be able to find relief from this burning need.

"You're a good girl for asking first. But no." She groaned in disappointment as he put the car into reverse.

"Daddy, please!" she cried but he only

shook his head.

"Not until we get home, little one. That doesn't mean you can stop playing with yourself, though. Put on your seatbelt, and then I want you to edge all the way home. And then, you're going to get it, little one."

Chapter 11

Hannah somehow managed to hold on until they pulled into Paul's driveway.

"Get inside, little one. Daddy has been waiting for this all day." She practically skipped to his front door, eager to end her torture at last. As he opened the door, she noticed that he had an armful of shopping bags.

"What's that?" she asked curiously, suddenly remembering his promise of presents.

"Nevermind, I'll show you later," he said, putting them down by the door. "Now get on your knees and show Daddy how much you missed me."

"I missed so much, Daddy," she said, kneeling before him obediently.

"I missed you too, pumpkin." He smiled down at her and pulled his cock out, stroking it slowly as she watched with greedy fascination.

"Now open that pretty little mouth." Eagerly, she opened wide, moaning happily at the taste of him as he slid his erection on to her soft, wet tongue.

"I've been thinking about this hot little mouth all day," he groaned and grabbed the back of her head firmly. Holding her in place, he eased his cock further down her throat until she began to gag. She remembered to look up at him as he penetrated her throat. Her pussy was dripping wet as she enjoyed the look of ecstasy on his handsome face, knowing how much pleasure she was bringing him. He stroked her face tenderly as he forced his cock deeper down her throat, smiling at the way she choked on him, whispering encouragement as he pushed her to her limits.

"That's it, baby. Keep that mouth open, let Daddy fuck that pretty little face" he said as he pulled out. Drool dribbled down her chin and chest, staining her swimsuit. He smiled down at her, enjoying the sight of her getting dirty to please him.

"Did you like choking on my cock, baby

girl?" She nodded, obediently keeping her mouth open. He placed the head of his cock on her tongue again but didn't push in. "Do you want some more?"

"Uh-huh," she nodded again.

"Good girl," he growled, and he thrust himself deep into her throat. She moaned and gurgled as he slid down her throat, his thick erection cutting off her air supply. As she held her breath, she noticed how it intensified every sensation and made her pussy ache for relief. He began to pull back, but she grabbed his hips, not wanting to let go just yet. He watched with loving fascination as she struggled to keep him down. He pulled out just as she was beginning to get light-headed and stroked his cock, watching her gasp for air.

"You're such a good little cocksucker, aren't you baby girl?" he asked, wiping a bit of drool from her chin. She nodded and swallowed.

"Yes, Daddy. I love sucking your cock." She was glowing with pride at his praise, proud to be a good slut for him.

"Good girl," he purred. "You're so sexy, little one. I love watching you choke on me. Ready for some more?"

"Yes, please," she grinned and opened her mouth wide. He sank his cock in, even deeper than before. She relaxed into it, so lost in her haze of lust and obedience that she swallowed him completely. He set a hypnotizing pace, fucking her throat slowly but steadily. The rougher he got, the more her pussy tingled and dripped with desire. She kept my hands at her sides even though she ached to cum with his cock down her throat. She swallowed his cock over and over, hoping that she would earn the privilege of cumming soon.

"Oh, princess, you're going to make me cum. Are you going to be a good girl and swallow it?"

"Yes, Daddy," she squealed with delight. "I want to swallow all of your yummy cum!" With a grunt, he thrust himself down her throat, and she opened wide as she felt his cock pulse. He shouted as he came and pushed himself deeper still into her throat. She struggled not to choke and managed to swallow every bit of it down just as she had promised.

"Oh, baby," he said, gently pulling himself out of her mouth. "You're such a good girl, I'm so proud of you."

"Thank you, Daddy," she said.

"I think you've earned yourself an orgasm, little one. Why don't you take off that swimsuit and come sit on Daddy's face." She quickly shed her suit, eager to have the chance to finally cum at last. He led her over to the couch, lying on his back and pulling her on top of him so that she was straddling his face. He gave her pussy a long slow lick, moaning with delight as he tasted her. She moaned with relief as he finally gave her aching pussy the attention it had been begging and ground her hips against him. He grabbed her by the wrists and moved her hands to her bare breasts.

"Play with those perfect titties, kitten," he

whispered. "Give Daddy a little show." He went back to twirling his tongue around her clit as she obeyed, pinching her nipples as he watched her closely.

"Harder," he commanded. "I know you can take it." She twisted her nipple as hard as she could, the pain combining with the delicious sensations of his tongue lapping at her and she moaned, grinding herself against his mouth. His fingers dug into the flesh of her ass as he devoured her, bringing another layer of delightful sensation.

"Slap your tits," he growled and flicked his tongue lightly across her clit. Tentatively, she smacked her palms on her nipples, intrigued by the sensation. "Harder. I want to watch your tits get as red as your ass." She slapped her breasts with more and more force, each time the pain mixed with pleasure brought her closer to a climax. He groaned approvingly and smack her ass hard, almost making her lose control.

"Please, Daddy," she cried out. "Please I need to cum so bad!"

"I know, baby girl. You can cum for Daddy now." She moaned with sweet relief as she squirmed against his mouth. He brought his hand down onto her fleshy buttock once more, and she could hold back no longer. Instinctively, she twisted her nipples, harder than ever before as she came, wave after wave of intense pleasure washing over her. He held her firmly down on his tongue as she shivered and quaked, her moans echoing off through the entire house. As she collapsed back, he caught her, gently easing her down on the couch. She sighed happily as he kissed her deeply. She could taste her own juices on his tongue, and she moaned into his mouth, feeling delightfully naughty. She loved the way she never felt inhibited around him, the way he was opening her up to a whole new world of pleasure. To her surprise, Paul was already hard again. Eating her out must have aroused him once more because she could feel him begin to press into her, ready to claim her again. With a sigh, he grabbed her by the hips and flipped her so that she was up on all fours. She was still sensitive from her climax and shivered with ecstasy as he thrust into her. She moaned and pushed back to meet him, taking him deeper inside of her, still craving more of him. She didn't think she would ever get enough of him.

"Daddy, you feel so good," she cried out, thrashing her head against the pillow as he split her open again and again. He grabbed her hand, guiding it to touch her clit as he pounded into her.

"Do you want to cum again, princess?" he asked.

"Yes, Daddy," she said, rubbing her clit frantically as his hard cock stretched her out.

"Oh princess, you're milking my cock so good. You're so tight and wet, just for me, isn't that right?"

"Just for you, Daddy," she agreed.

"That's right, Daddy's little greedy slut who just wants to cum on his cock, again and again, right kitten?"

"Yes, Daddy. I want to cum on your cock. Can I, please?"

"Yes, baby girl. You've been such a good slut for Daddy today. You can cum again if you want to." She couldn't answer, she could only moan and rub her clit as she clenched around his cock, climaxing with such force that her legs shook.

"Good girl," he growled and hammered into her even harder. As the waves of ecstasy, receded she pulled her hand away from her clit, but that earned her a hard slap on the ass, making her yelp with pain. He roughly grabbed her by the wrist and replaced her hand between her legs.

"I didn't tell you to stop touching yourself, now did I baby girl?" he growled, smacking her ass again. Hannah's eyes rolled back in her head, the thoughts in her head thoroughly scrambled.

"N-no, Daddy," she managed to stammer out. Obediently, she ran her finger over her swollen clit once again, overwhelmed with pleasure as he claimed her body with his.

"You did such a good job holding back, but now I don't want you to stop cumming until you can't think or stand." She shivered as the image made her toes curl. Already, she felt unable to form words or thoughts. As she grunted and thrust back against him, she felt more like her true self than she ever had before. It felt so right and natural to give over control to him, to be his slave made only to please him. The thought made her pussy clench, and she knew that she would soon be orgasming again, just as he had commanded.

"Oh Daddy," she squealed and came so hard that her voice broke, and her legs collapsed beneath her. Paul just kept right on fucking her into the couch without mercy. She kicked her legs and squealed, the stimulation was too much to handle, and she felt like she was losing her mind.

"Such a good slut," He groaned and swatted her ass again. "Keep rubbing that clit, little one. I'm not going to tell you again." Hannah obeyed at once, not wanting to find out what was behind that veiled threat. She rubbed her clit, helpless against the onslaught of pleasure as Paul continued to use her roughly, just the way she liked it. She whined and moaned, her skin growing slick with sweat as she thrashed and kicked underneath him. No one had ever fucked her so thoroughly before, had certainly never engaged her mind or emotions as they fucked her the way that he did. As overstimulated as she felt, she also didn't want it to end. Just as she was beginning to think that she couldn't handle cumming one more time, she could feel Paul stiffening inside of her, and she knew that he was about to go over the edge again.

"Oh baby girl, you're doing so good, keep taking it just like that," he cried out, grabbing a fist full of her hair for purchase as he slammed into her. The pain in her scalp combined with the hot cum he was pumping into her pussy made her shake with an orgasm so powerful that she couldn't even make noise. She could only shiver and quake beneath him. It seemed to last forever, but at last, she collapsed against the couch, utterly spent. He, too, collapsed onto the couch, curling himself around her as they regained their breath. *He got his wish;* she thought to herself as the idea of moving or even thinking seemed impossible.

She felt like her entire body had turned to jelly. She was sore and exhausted but also happier than she had ever felt in her life. Paul wrapped his arm around her waist, pulling her close.

"Oh princess, you are so perfect. Daddy is so proud of you." He held her face up to his for a kiss, his warm lips gentle and soft against hers. She melted into him, savoring the warm feeling of skin on skin.

Chapter 12

Eventually, he disentangled himself from her with a groan, stretching languidly before getting up to grab the shopping bags that were still waiting by the door.

"Are you ready for your presents, little one?" He set the bags in front of her, and she could feel the energy returning to her limbs as if by magic. She sat up on the couch and clapped her hands excitedly.

"Yes!" she cried. "Gimme, gimme." He laughed and picked up one of the bags and set it on her lap.

"Go ahead," he prompted, and she tore into the bag to find a treasure trove of stuffed animals, coloring books and crayons, and pacifiers for her to enjoy. "I wanted to pick up a few things that you can leave here. I want to make sure that you feel completely at home when you sleepover." She felt her heart melt as she looked from the pile of toys to his warm, sincere eyes. She reached out and touched his face, suddenly wanting to make sure that he was real and that all of this hadn't been just a beautiful dream.

"I love it. I do feel at home here with you." He smiled and grabbed her hand, pulling it to his lips for a tender kiss.

"Glad to hear it," he said, his voice thick with emotion. He stood and scooped her up from the couch, making her squeal and giggle as he swung her up into his arms. "Come on, let's get you diapered up, and you can play while I make us dinner." He carried her to the bedroom and placed her gently on the bed. He took a moment to admire her as she opened her legs for him.

"Fuck, baby girl, you look so sexy with my cum leaking out of you. You couldn't be any more perfect." He took a wet wipe and began to delicately clean her off, moving it slowly over her pussy as his breath began to quicken. It filled her with such pride, knowing that he was already hungry for her again, even after she had pleasured him so many times. He slid a fresh diaper under her and fastened it with elastic tabs.

"I have an old t-shirt you can wear," he said, going into his closet to select one for her. "I suppose we'll have to bring some extra clothes over here as well." She giggled. "That reminds me, we'd better wash that bathing suit before I go back to work tomorrow after we got it so dirty." He smirked and tossed her a clean t-shirt. "I suppose you're right. Totally worth it, though."

"Totally worth it," she agreed, sliding his t-shirt over her head and standing up. His eyes lit up as he looked at her.

"You can keep all the fancy lingerie in the world," he said, looking her up and down admiringly. "You've never looked more beautiful and sexy than you do right now. I wish you could always just be in a diaper and my shirt." He grabbed her by the ass, patting her diapered behind lovingly, making her giggle and blush. He picked her up once again and carried her into the living room and put her down on the floor. She loved the way he carried her around all the time. It made her feel so little and protected. He fished around in the bag for a pacifier and placed it gently in her mouth, then laid her coloring supplies and a couple of stuffies on the floor next to her. He watched her play for a few minutes, helping her decide the names of new stuffed animal friends, before wandering off to the kitchen to make their dinner.

***

"I have another surprise for you," he said over dinner, making her eyes go wide in surprise.

"Another one?!" He laughed and took her hand, squeezing it affectionately.

"I got the call today that your car is finally ready. I was beginning to worry that it wouldn't be ready until after your graduation ceremony, but we can pick it up tomorrow. When is your graduation, by the way?"

"In three days, the day after my interview come to think of it." Her brow wrinkled with worry as she began to remember all of her real-life responsibilities. Interviews had always made her nervous, even when they were just the kind of low paying jobs that had put her through school. Now that she was faced with interviewing for her dream job, her stomach curdled with anxiety. Paul saw her expression change and reached out for her hand again. His touch did soothe her, she noticed.

"Hey," he said softly. "You have nothing to worry about. They're going to love you just as much as I do." Her face turned red, but she did feel calmer after his reassuring words. She smiled and tried to put the worry out of her mind.

"Thank you, Daddy," she said softly.

"What would you like to do to celebrate your new job? Big party?" He winked, knowing full well how little she liked parties. She laughed and shook her head.

"Absolutely nothing," she said. "I've been working for so hard and for so long that all I want now is a day where I do absolutely nothing."

"Done," he said. "Call in sick to work tomorrow. I'll wait on you hand and foot. You won't have to lift a finger for the whole day." She looked at him, completely surprised that he had taken her joke so seriously.

"Really?" The thought was tempting, sure, but she couldn't expect him to do everything for her for an entire day, could she?

"Really and truly," he said. "Let me take care of you. I want to, and you deserve it."

"Ok," she said with a grin. "I'll let Mr. Williams know right away." She took out her phone to type out a text, but he took it from her hands.

"Actually, let's not wait for tomorrow. Starting now, I'll take care of everything you need, including texting your boss. All you have to worry about is coming up with things for me to get you or do for you. Or to you." He winked again and turned his attention to typing out the message. Once again, she found herself wondering what she could have done to deserve such a wonderful man. It seemed impossible to her that he could be so aggressive in the bedroom and so kind to her the rest of the time. She didn't think she could have created a more perfect man if she had tried.

"All set," he said with a grin, handing her phone back to her. "What is your first command, my princess?"

"Read me a story!" she said, naming the first thing that popped into her head.

"I seem to recall a certain book that you were going to borrow. Want me to read you that one?" She nodded, getting even more excited at the idea. She had gotten so wrapped up in the events of the past few days that she had completely forgotten about that book.

"Ok, princess, let's go upstairs." He picked her up from the table and carried her to the bedroom. He placed her gently on the bed and then went to fetch the book. After tucking her in, he snuggled up next to her on the bed and found the page that she had marked when she had last read it.

"No, go back some, I don't remember what happened," she said.

"Yes, ma'am," he said and went back to the beginning of the chapter. She lay back and closed her eyes, listening to his deep, velvety voice. She stifled a yawn, not wanting to admit even to herself that she was sleepy. She wanted to listen to him read forever. Try as she might; however, she couldn't fight off sleep as the exhaustion from a long day at work on top of their marathon lovemaking finally caught up with her. Paul waited until her breaths were long and even to make sure that she was asleep before he slipped out of bed as quietly as he could to go clean up the kitchen.

Chapter 13

She awoke sometime later to something brushing between her legs. She opened her eyes to see Paul putting his hand down her diaper. She moaned and opened her legs, ready for him in an instant. He kissed her as he fingered her pussy, further igniting her desire.

"You're already wet," he noted with satisfaction. "You just need more of Daddy's cock."

"I sure do, Daddy. That is definitely next on my princess list." She ran her fingers through his silky black hair as he twirled his tongue around hers. Impatiently, he ripped her diaper off her and tossed it aside. As he settled between her legs, she noted that he was already naked and ready for her. He began to trail sloppy kisses down her neck and breasts, working his way down her body until his face was buried between her legs. With a happy sigh, he gave her pussy a long, slow lick, twirling his tongue sensually around her swollen clit. She threw her head back against the pillow and moaned as he expertly pleasured her.

"That's it, pumpkin," he said, sliding a finger into her. "Let Daddy take care of this needy little pussy." He resumed his attention to her clit. He reached his free hand up to grab her breast and pinched her nipple as she had done earlier. They were still sore from the abuse she had inflicted on them, and it stung all the more as he squeezed them harder and harder. The combined sensations of pleasure and pain drew her closer to orgasm, and she squirmed against his mouth, not sure how much leeway her princess day would allow her. She whined and kicked her legs, holding herself back just in case. Just then, he stopped and repositioned himself so that he was on top of her, his hardness pressing against her aching pussy. He kissed her deeply as his hands circled her wrists, holding them down onto the mattress gently but firmly. She loved it when he held her down like that, keeping her in place as his cock slowly worked its way into position. She loved being reminded of his control over her.

"Do you like cumming on Daddy's cock, little one?" he asked sweetly, pressing himself against her entrance.

"I love cumming on your cock, Daddy. It feels so good when you fuck me."

"I'm glad to hear it. Since it's your princess day, you can cum whenever you like, ok pumpkin?"

"Oh, thank you, Daddy," she moaned as he inched his cock inside of her. "You're so good to me." She nearly sang with delight as he began to sink his cock further inside of her, still holding her firmly down by the wrists. He entered her so painfully slow that she tried to thrust her hips upwards to take more of him in, but he had his weight positioned so that she couldn't move. No matter which way she squirmed, she was pinned in place beneath him. He continued that excruciatingly slow pace until he was buried inside of her completely, holding himself there for a moment before pulling out again at that same incredibly slow speed.

"Daddy," she whined, futilely kicking her legs. "What are you doing?"

"What do you mean," he said, his voice heavy with fake innocence. "You asked for Daddy's cock, so I'm letting you have it." She groaned as he sank back into her, filling her up inch by excruciating inch.

"Please," she cried out "I need you to fuck me!"

"But sweetheart, I am fucking you." His voice still had that fake, syrupy-sweet innocence as though he had no idea that she was on the verge of tears, desperate for the hard pounding she beginning to grow accustomed to.

"Please, Daddy," she said, thrashing my head back and forth on the pillow. His slow torture was too much, and she felt like she might explode. "I need you to fuck me hard. I need you to pound me with your cock. Pound my pussy, Daddy. Give it to me!"

"Your wish is my command, princess," he said with a happy growl and unleashed himself onto her. Still holding her down by the wrists, he finally gave her the fucking that she had begged for. He pounded into her so hard and fast that every thrust made her go mad with pleasure. She did not last long, coming undone beneath him. She grabbed his hips and held on as her body seized with ecstasy. He growled and pumped into her even more furiously as she clenched around him. Even as she relaxed against the sheets, her orgasm waning, he did not lessen his pace. His breath grew faster, panting and growling in her ear as the onslaught of pleasure continued. She could still feel waves of pleasure with every wild thrust, almost like aftershocks. She knew that if he kept fucking her this way, she would be cumming again very soon. She loved seeing him unleashed like this, loved knowing that she made him lose control. He released her hands so that he could grab her breasts, squeezing them so tightly that she gasped.

"I love how tight you get when I do that. Daddy's greedy little pain slut." His words made her tighten around him even more, and she could feel his muscles begin to tense, knew that he was getting closer to his climax as well. As he drove himself deep inside of her with one final thrust, she exploded around him. He flooded her pussy with his hot cum waves of pure joy and ecstasy overtook her. They shouted as they came together and fell back in a panting, sweaty heap.

"Oh baby girl," he whispered and pulled her close. "You're so much more than I ever could have dreamed of. I'm so glad I found you." He held her and kissed her for a while until she began to yawn again. It had grown dark as she slept, and she wondered vaguely what time it was.

"Get some more sleep, princess. I'll be right here when you wake up."

Chapter 14

The rest of her princess day went by in a happy daze, as though she were living in a beautiful dream. Paul served her a huge breakfast in bed, even going to far as to feed her one bite at a time. There were eggs, toast, coffee, and fruit, so much that she couldn't even finish it all.

"I told you you weren't going to lift a finger today, and I meant it," he had said as he fed her fork full after fork full. After breakfast, they lay in bed for a while, just cuddling and chatting. Eventually, he diapered her and carried her downstairs so that they could watch cartoons on the couch. As they relaxed, she got an email informing her that she had aced her last final and would be graduating with honors after all. Paul insisted on cracking open a bottle of champagne in celebration of the wonderful news despite the early hour. She giggled as the bubbles tickled her nose, and it really did seem as though she were living in a dream, a happy dream that she hoped she never woke up from. The bubbly alcohol only added to her giddiness, and she giggled at nothing like a mad woman. They made a picnic on the floor for lunch. Paul put together a simple meal of sandwiches and orange slices. After they ate, they made love again, their fingers and lips still sticky from the citrus fruit. Her body ached from so much lovemaking but still, she wanted more of him. Afterward, she colored on the floor while he read on the couch, both of them enjoying the quiet time together. Later that afternoon, he drove her to her house so that she could prepare for her interview. He quizzed her with mock interview questions as she modeled various outfits for him. Eventually, she settled on one and laid it out for the morning. Once she felt thoroughly prepared for the interview, he insisted that she get into bed early so that she would be nice and rested the next morning.

"I thought it was my princess day and that I could do anything I wanted," she objected. He kissed her nose.

"It may be your princess day, but Daddy is still in charge, understood?"

"Yes, Daddy," she conceded. "But I'm not sleepy yet."

"Do you want me to bring you some dinner?" he offered, but she shook her head.

"No, I think I'm too nervous to eat."

"Hmm," he thought for a moment before pulling out his phone. "I think I have just the thing." A few taps later, he pulled up a soothing music playlist, complete with babbling brooks and chirping birds. He set that off the side and then scooped her up into his lap, rocking her gently as he held her. She closed her eyes, relaxing into his warm embrace.

"It's all going to be ok, little one. You are going to get this job. I just know it. You're the smartest, sweetest girl I've ever met, and they'd be absolutely insane not to hire you. So just rest your little head and quit worrying." The rocking motion was incredibly soothing, and his embrace was so warm. She felt so safe in his arms that the nervousness began to melt away. Surprisingly, she could feel sleep begin to creep up on her as he stroked her hair.

***

"Wake up, little one," he whispered in her ear. "It's time to rise and shine." She opened her eyes to see that it was already morning somehow.

"How did you do that?" she asked blearily. "The last thing I remember, you were rocking me."

"Daddy magic," he grinned, looking very proud of himself. "Now, get up and get dressed. I'll have breakfast waiting on you when you're done." She dragged herself reluctantly from under the covers and padded to the bathroom to get ready. True to his word, he had a full breakfast of pancakes and coffee waiting on the table.

"You look so beautiful, kitten," he said,

pulling out a chair for her to sit in. "Very professional." She had chosen a navy pantsuit and a plain white button-up, far more conservative than her usual shorts and swimsuits, and it felt strange.

"I'm not sure I can eat. I'm still really nervous."

"You'd better eat, young lady," he said firmly. "You're not going to that interview on an empty stomach, not on my watch. I'll feed you again if I have to." She giggled and threw her hands up in mock surrender.

"Alright, alright," she said. "I'll eat." After the first bite, she realized how ravenous she was and wolfed the rest of it down, gulping her coffee between bites. Within minutes, she had completely cleaned her plate. He insisted on driving her to her interview, saying that he wanted to be there when she got the good news. She smiled at his optimism, hoping that it was warranted. He held her hand the whole way there, and she was so grateful to have him by her side. No matter how the interview went, she at least had Paul. The interview was awkward at first, but as the conversation turned to the animals she would be caring for, her favorite subject in the whole world, she lit up. She felt more like herself, and the answers came easily. By the end of it, it felt like she and Mr. Chance were chatting like old friends. She did her best to keep her poker face on as she came out into the waiting room where Paul was waiting for her, wanting to keep him in suspense as he so often did to her.

"Well," he asked impatiently. "How did it go?" She broke out into a grin, unable to hold it back any longer.

"They want me to start next week," she said. He whooped with joy and wrapped his arms around her, swinging her around with unencumbered glee.

"See?" he laughed and kissed her on the lips. "I told you you'd get the job. I just knew you would be able to. Daddy is always right, remember that, little one. Unless I am wrong in which I will apologize, but I am mostly always right." She laughed along with him, her heart overflowing with joy.

"I will. Now, let's get out of here."

Chapter 15

They decided to spend the night at her place again.

"Wait right here," she said, as they came inside. She rushed off to her bedroom to find a silky nightgown, stripping off her suit and underwear. She pulled the black, lacy material down over her naked body. Wanting to make sure that she looked as good as possible, she ran her fingers through her hair, biting her lips slightly until they were pink and swollen and pinched her cheeks, a trick she had seen in an old movie. As she came back into the living room, the look on Paul's face was absolutely priceless as he stared at her in stunned silence.

"I know it's no diaper and t-shirt, but do you think this will do?" He nodded slowly, his wide eyes glued to the curves of her body. She crooked a finger at him, motioning for him to follow, then walked back to the bedroom. Behind her, she could hear the soft rustle of his shirt being pulled overhead followed by the quiet jingle of his pant being undone. She smiled quietly to herself at his eagerness. He caught up with her as they entered her room, his hands circling her waist and stopping her forward momentum. He touched her greedily, running his palms over the silky material of her negligee, relishing the warm softness of her flesh underneath. Her eyes fluttered closed, and she could feel the smile pulling at his lips as he brushed her long hair aside and kissed the curve where her neck and shoulder meet. Letting herself go, she freely moaned and writhed against him, stoking the fire. She pressed her backside against his growing erection, shivering as he bit her neck in response. The pain made her blood go hot, and he moaned as he sensed her heightened arousal, his breath moist and warm against her skin. He yanked the skirt of her negligee up, running his hands over the bare skin of her hips and stomach. She reached back and pulled him closer, leaning her head back on his chest as he enjoyed her body. His hands wandered upwards towards her breasts, cupping them gently and caressing her nipples lightly with his fingertips. The sensations took her breath away. The heady desire made her feel dizzy as he dug his fingernails into her tender skin. She gasped as the pain brought her sharply into the here and now, filling her with a frantic need. Impatient with lust, Amber lifted the negligee the rest of the way over her head and lie down on the bed, face down, hips lifted invitingly. He joined her, straddling her legs as he began to paint her back with delicate kisses. His cock was nestled between the warm soft flesh of her buttocks. Every small movement of her hips made him want to plunge himself inside of her, but he held back, sensing she was in the mood for a long, slow fuck. He lowered his weight onto her, gathering up her long hair so that he could access the curve of her neck. Working his way around with his tongue, he nipped the spot where her spine met her skull sending electric shivers throughout her entire being. Her back arched and she let out a deep guttural moan. He let his hands wander over the generous swell of her hips and buttocks. He shifted his legs to part hers and settled between them, seeking out the burning core of her desire. He ran his fingers lightly over her pubic hairs, tickling and teasing her sex, making her squirm pleasingly beneath her. His teasing fingers moved inward, teasing her folds and the hood of her clit, the light touch on her most sensitive parts driving her wild with need. She kicked her feet to expel some of the galvanizing energy dancing along her skin.

"Oh, we're just get started, my dear," he whispered, his breath hot against her ear.

"You're not going to get any relief for quite some time." Her agonized groan was music to his ears. She strained her hips backward, seeking more stimulation and he obliged, slipping a finger between her folds to discover the wetness pooling there.

"Oh my, you're a horny little thing, aren't you?" He circled her aching entrance, knowing just how much she longed to be filled, to be penetrated, but he wasn't ready to give her the satisfaction just yet. Instead, he smacked her ass firmly, watching it jiggle from the impact. He liked watching it so much, he did it again and again, until her pale flesh began to turn pink. Each impact stoked her passion all the more, her squeals and moans began to take on a pleading tone.

"What's wrong? Did you want my fingers inside of you again?" He stopped spanking her and went back to teasing her dripping slit.

"Yes, Daddy. Please!" she gasped out, already knowing it wouldn't be that easy.

"Unh-unh," he chimed in a sing-song tone. He traced a line of kisses down her spine, lifting her up by the hips and tilted her pelvis forward until he could bury his face in her fragrant pussy. His tongue explored and tasted her, deliberately avoiding the spots that gave her the most pleasure. He didn't let up until she was a quivering, dripping mess that could only emit a high-pitched whine, begging him me to fill her up, to fuck her hard, to use her over and over. Having finally gotten her to the desired level of desperation, he slowly slipped the tip of one finger into her, smiling to himself as she thrust her hips back, trying to take him deeper. He didn't give her more than his fingertip, however, no matter how she angled herself.

The lust and need had completely clouded her mind. All conscious thought had melted away leaving behind a mindless, rutting animal in heat, desperate to mounted. She was an aching void that needed to be filled, to be tamed, to be mastered. At last, she accepted his control over her pleasure, surrendering to the teasing torment of his fingertip. Feeling her give in, he rewarded her by plunging his finger inside of her, giving her the full penetration she needed so badly. With his free hand, he once again spanked her pink and tender bottom. As he worked his finger in and out of her, she got so lost in the steady rhythm of pain and pleasure that she edged dangerously close to an orgasm.

"Not yet, my pet," he whispered,

withdrawing his finger from her despite her greedy whimpers of protest. "Let's put that wet little mouth of yours to work, shall we?" He lie down on the bed, putting his hands behind his head so that he could better watch his sexy little fuck slave work her magic. Obediently, she got on all fours between his legs, then lowered herself down to her elbows with her ass up in the air like a playful puppy. Maintaining eye contact, she wrapped her lips around his swollen cock and swallowed him down her seemingly endless throat in one long, agonizingly slow motion. Once he was enveloped in her tight, warm throat entirely, she caressed his balls with her silky, cool fingertips. He almost came down her throat right then but just barely managed to hold himself back. She stilled herself until he regained his self-control, then began to face fuck herself with his cock, pushing past her own gag reflex to take his cock deeper and faster. He stroked her cheeks and hair as she serviced him, showing her how proud he was of her and how sexy she was to him. He watched her ass wiggle in the air as she bobbed her head up and down on his erection, slurping and moaning happily as she devoted herself entirely to his pleasure. Swallowing his cock made her feel strangely whole, as well as incredibly horny. Once again, she had to slow her pace so that he could retain his composure. Still too close to the edge, he pulled her off his dick by a fist full of hair, pulling her towards him until her perky breasts swung in his face. Capturing her nipple in his mouth, he sucked on it hard, delighting in the pain that shot through her and the way it made her grind her hot mound against his stomach. He scooted her hips down until his cock was resting against the cleft of her ass.

"Please, Daddy," she whined, rubbing her moist slit up the length of his hardness. "Please fuck me. I need to feel you inside of me." He spread her cheeks, teasing her entrance with the tip of his cock while he worked her nipple between her teeth. Slowly, he let himself slip inside of her, inching his way into her tight wetness. Her eyes rolled back as he, at last, filled her needy cunt. As he thrust into her, waves of pleasure came crashing down on her, and she was filled with the urgent need to cum.

"Daddy, please let me cum on your cock," she whined. He watched her riding him, looking so beautiful as her head rolled back, lost in ecstasy.

"Yes, princess. Cum on Daddy's cock like a good slut." She shuddered and twitched on top of him, lost in her own boundless universe of ecstasy. Her legs quivered and shook around him as she came, but he was far from satisfied with just one. He knew from experience that she had many more where that came from and he was going to fuck them all out of her. Her first orgasm left her all the more sensitive, so as he parted her thighs further so that he could penetrate her deeper, she could only throw her head back and try to hold on as he split her open. Gathering her wrists in his hands and forcing them behind her back, he battered her tender pussy, wanting to torture her with pleasure. He wrapped one hand around both of her delicate wrists and the other around her slender throat. As he squeezed, she relished the heady mixture of helplessness and trust that washed over her as she leaned into his hand, silently encouraging him to squeeze harder.

"Cum for me again, princess," he commanded, knowing that she was already getting close once more. She rode his cock in a slow and steady rhythm, her universe narrowed down to warm hardness stretching and filling her and his large, rough hands dominating her body. Another orgasm ripped through her, stronger than the first, his hardness thrusting into her with no mercy as she stiffened, her lips wordlessly moving. As her climax waned, he released her throat but not her hands.

Regaining her breath, she moaned loudly, her inhibitions totally melted away. She let herself surrender to the pounding between her legs, lost in an ocean of pleasure and submission. For his part, Paul was content to watch her bounce up and down on his cock. With her hands behind her back, it forced her chest forward, and her perfect tits bounced with every thrust. He reached up and grabbed a fistful of her hair, forcing her head back, exaggerating the effect even more.

"You are so fucking sexy. My sweet little fuckdoll. Mine. Mine. Mine." He slammed himself deep inside of her with every "mine." It felt so fucking good to be claimed by him, to feel like she belonged and that she was desirable. She couldn't get enough of fucking him, of cumming on his cock, of being his. He shifted on the small bed, gently guiding her to all fours as he knelt behind her. He took a moment to enjoy the view, her thighs and round ass parted slightly to reveal her glistening sex, slick with her orgasms. With a soft growl, he gave her a hard spank and entered her from behind. She dropped down to her elbows, allowing him to go deeper. As he gripped her hips and thrust into her, they were both soon lost in the ancient rhythm of grunts and thrust and moans. They existed outside of time, his desire stoking hers as hers did his, both with an endless hunger they never wanted to be sated. He grabbed her hand, guiding it to her clit.

"You're going to make Daddy cum, and I want you to cum with me, got that princess?

"Yes Daddy," she gasped, working her clit furiously as he pounded into her. Once again, he grabbed a fistful of her hair, forcing her head back. The pain sent her over the edge, and she screamed as she came. As her pussy pulsed around him, he couldn't hold on any longer and released himself inside of her. As he lay on the mattress, beside her, he found her hand and brought it to his lips for a kiss. She snuggled close to him, laying her head on his chest and listened to his pounding heart.

Chapter 16

Finally, graduation day arrived. She Skyped with her Mom who was unable to get away from work and unable to afford the ticket from the mainland anyway. Hannah was happy just to see her face and hear her voice. It had been quite some time since they had seen each other.

"I can't believe my baby is graduating with honors," her mom cried. "You've worked so hard for so long. I'm so proud of you." She introduced Paul to her Mom while she had her on video chat. Even though they had technically only been together for a very short period of time, she knew that this was the man for her, and she wanted the whole world to know it. Her mother seemed thoroughly charmed by him, almost as charmed as Hannah was. The graduation ceremony was short and sweet. It wasn't a very large school, so Hannah was only one of a few students getting their diplomas that day. Afterward, she was taking a few celebratory selfies with her classmates when she saw Paul carrying a bouquet of flowers and a gift bag, scanning the crowd for her. She waved him down and crossed the crowd to meet him. Paul handed her the flowers, and she blushed, sniffing them discreetly.

"I got you another graduation present," he said, holding up the gift bag. "But, you might want to open this one in private." She blushed even deeper and looked around her shyly, wondering what it could be.

"Just let me know when you're done here, and I'll take you back to my place." She slid her hand into his, ready to follow him anywhere.

"I'm ready now," she said. "Let's go."

***

Back at his place, she opened his other present eagerly. Inside was a small velvet box, like a jewelry box. Inside was a silver pacifier with "Daddy's Girl" engraved into it. She examined it more closely to find that it was a fully functioning pacifier, complete with a rubber tip.

"Oh Daddy, I love it," she exclaimed, slipping it in her mouth to try it out.

"I'm so glad," he said. "I wanted to give you something that showed you how much you mean to me. I'm so grateful to have you in my life. I know that we've only been together a short time but, Hannah, I love you." She stared at him in shock as the words sank in. Her jaw went so slack that the pacifier fell right out and into her lap.

"You make me so happy, baby girl,' he continued. "Happier than I've ever been before, happier than I ever could have dreamed. You're all I've ever wanted. I used to dream about what it would be like to have someone to come home to, someone to protect and look after. Now that I have you, it's better than I ever could have imagined it. You don't have to say it back if it's too early."

"I love you too," she said quietly,

interrupting him. He smiled at her in happy relief.

"You do? Oh pumpkin, that's fantastic."

"Of course I do. I'm absolutely crazy about you, Paul." He kissed her softly on the lips and pulled her close against him. Very quickly, their kisses grew more heated, and they fell back onto the couch. He moaned into her mouth as their tongues meet, grinding his already hard cock against her needy sex. He pulled the straps of her dress down and captured her nipple with his teeth, teasing her and watching her writhe beneath him. He squeezed her breasts together and buried his face in her cleavage, licking and nibbling hungrily. She suddenly ached to feel his skin against her and pulled at his shirt, whining with impatience as he pulled it over his head. As he settled back on top of her, she ran her hands over the muscles of his back. Their naked flesh pressed together as he kissed her again. He lifted up the skirt of her dress and growled with approval when he sees that she's not wearing any panties, a little surprise just for him.

"So naughty, little one," he said with a grin and lowered himself between her legs. With a deep breath in to savor her scent, he teased her lightly with his tongue. She gripped her thighs, holding her legs wide open as he continued to explore her dripping folds. He moaned as he tasted her, working his way inward, seeking out her clit. She whimpered as he twirled his tongue around her sensitive spot, her legs began to quiver as he picked up speed. He sank a finger into her tight pussy, watching how it made her squirm, then a second finger, stretching her out as she gasped and moaned. His fingers pumped in and out of her as his tongue traced circles of ecstasy over her clit. She already felt a powerful orgasm building, but she held off, waiting for his permission like a good girl. Finally, he stopped pleasuring her long enough to pull her dress the rest of the way off. He pulled the rest of his clothes off as well, freeing his rock hard cock. She stared at it longingly, watching it as he stroked it seductively, her expression get hungrier by the minute.

"Turn over, princess," he said. "Get that sexy ass in the air." His voice was gruff and commanding, making her body thrill with arousal. Eagerly, she rolled onto her tummy, sticking her ass straight up just as he instructed. She waited like that as he looked at her for a long while and continued to pleasure himself. Her pussy was throbbing, but she waited obediently for what would come next. As always, the anticipation only heightened her desire for him. He smacked her ass hard enough to make her pussy tingle. She moaned as he spanked her again and again until her cheeks burned. Once he was satisfied with how pink her ass cheeks had gotten, he grabbed her by the hair and brought her mouth to his cock. She opened for him eagerly as he thrust himself deep into her throat.

"That's it, baby," he moaned. "Suck it down deep like a good slut. Oh fuck, you're such a talented cocksucker." She moaned around his cock, loving the dirty way he talked to her when they fucked. He plunged his cock deeper, making her choke and drool. Every thrust down her throat made the ache in her pussy grow. The rougher he used her, the wilder it made her feel. He pulled out of her throat with a satisfied sigh and sat on the couch. He pulled her onto his lap so that she was straddling him. He bit down hard on her nipple, snickering at the way it made her writhe against him.

"Play with that needy pussy, baby," he muttered, pulling her cheeks apart before giving them a firm slap. "Show Daddy how badly you need this cock." She rubbed her clit frantically and ground her labia against his cock, so tantalizingly close to being inside of her. Even though he hadn't yet given her permission to cum, she felt herself getting dangerously close. He could tell from her frenzied moans that she was riding the line and grabbed a fistful of her hair to remind her of her place.

"Easy, little one," he growled. "If you cum without permission, I won't let you cum again for a whole week, understood?" She whimpered softly but slowed her pace.

"I understand, Daddy."

"Good girl." He pushed his cock toward her slick entrance, making her gasp with need.

"Who does this pussy belong to?"

"This pussy belongs to you," she cried out. He impaled her with his cock as a reward, making her eyes roll back as he buried himself inside of her in one swift thrust.

"That's right," he whispered. "Don't you fucking forget it, my precious little slut." Her back arched as he pounded into her, still playing with her clit. She moved hips to meet his, sliding up and down the length of him. She was on the edge of cumming on his cock as she rode him, gritting her teeth as she fought to stay in control.

"Mmm, my baby girl needs it badly, doesn't she?"

"Yes, Daddy! I need to cum so bad. Please, please, please ..." The words trailed off. She was so enraptured by lust that the words seemed to fail her. He laughed at her and twisted her nipples hard, making her gasp.

"Oh, I know you can do better than that, pumpkin. Beg like a good little, and Daddy might let you cum." She whimpered and slow down her pace, trying her best to focus. His cock was so distracting, though, and the pain in her nipples certainly didn't help.

"Please, Daddy. I want to cum on your cock so bad. I've been a good girl. Please let me cum. Your cock feels so good inside my slutty little pussy. Please, Daddy, can I?"

"Much better," he growled. He gripped her by the hips and flipped her onto her back, spreading her legs wide open as he rammed into her, hard and swift. "You can cum whenever you like, baby girl." He slammed into her, deep and furious. She rubbed her clit and wrapped her thighs around him, holding on tightly as her orgasm erupted. His head snapped back as the ecstasy to her, and she moaned with abandon. He had turned her into quite the screamer, she noted.

"That's right, sweetie, cum for Daddy. Just

like that. That's a good girl." He kissed her sweaty neck, and she tremble underneath him as he continued to fuck her. Shivers of pleasure ran through her even after the main wave passed. His thrusts did not slow in the least. He kept pounding into her, growling as he became wrapped up in his own pleasure.

"Oh, darling. You get so wet when you cum, did you know that? Such a sweet, dirty girl. You make Daddy's cock feel so good." She absolutely loved how vocal he got when he got close to cumming. She loved being reassured that she was his fantasy, his perfect girl. His muscles clenched. She knew that he was close, that her reward was coming any second now.

"Fuck yeah, baby girl. Keep taking Daddy's cock just like that. Oh, you're such a good girl. Daddy's good little slut. Here it comes, baby!" His body seized up, except for his cock, which pumped her full with his hot cum. With a groan, he collapsed against her, burying his head into her cleavage. He held her close to him, still inside of her, until he regained his breath. She kissed his sweaty forehead as she held him, a feeling of complete contentment washing over her. It seemed like a small miracle that they had found each other, that they completed one another so perfectly. She squeezed him tighter, hoping that she would be able to hold him like this forever.

Chapter 17

Three months later, Hannah awoke in her own bed with Paul sprawled out on the bed beside her, naked and snoring softly. She felt a wave of affection for him as she watched him sleep. As the next months rolled by, things between them only seemed to get better and better. They spent nearly every night together, and she had yet to grow tired of him, and she suspected that she never would. It was sort of an unwritten rule that whoever woke up first would wake the other one up with a little oral pleasure. It looked this morning. The privilege would be hers. As quietly as she could, she pulled the covers back and lowered herself until her face was level to his cock. Even soft, it was impressive to look at, laying across his toned belly, just waiting to spring to life. Slowly, she took the head into her mouth, gently applying pressure as she ran her tongue over the sensitive tip. He made a soft noise but didn't open his eyes just yet.

As she took him further into her mouth, she could feel his cock begin to stiffen as the blood flooded in. He still tasted of their shared juices from the night before, and she moaned lightly as she tasted him. He had gotten her addicted to the taste of her own pussy, associating it with the toe-curling pleasure he always gave her. As he grew harder, she began to apply more pressure, delighting in how responsive he was. His reactions made him a delight to pleasure. With a happy sigh, he finally opened his eyes and looked down at her with sleepy affection. He smiled and ran his fingers lightly through her hair as she worked his cock deeper into her throat.

"Good morning. Didn't get enough last night, huh little one?" he purred. "Mmm, I love how greedy you are for my cock." Grabbing a handful of her hair, he pushed her down further onto him, his partially erect member sliding easily down her throat. It was delightful, feeling a fullness in her throat without feeling like she had to gag, and she swallowed him greedily. He stroked her face as she pleasured him, getting harder and harder.

"Oh fuck, kitten!" Paul threw his head back against the pillow. "That's so good. Suck Daddy's cock." Hannah's body tingled with desire as she gagged and choked on him. She sucked him harder and faster, wanting to taste his cum, her favorite treat.

"Hold on, baby girl," he suddenly growled, pulling her up. She nearly whined with disappointment, but he cut it short by pulling her up for a deep kiss, fisting his hands into her hair. She straddled him and melted against him as his greedy tongue pushed into her mouth, his teeth lightly grazing her lip. "I'm not ready to cum just yet."

He pulled her hair and tugged her head to the side, exposing her neck. He held her like that as he kissed and bit her neck, making her squirm with desire. He knew just how to get her horny and desperate for him and did so as often as possible.

She gripped his broad shoulders as he devoured her neck, moaning softly as the mild pain in her scalp only intensified her need, craving more. She felt helpless pinned against him like that, and that helplessness was exhilarating. There was a tremendous amount of freedom in that helplessness for her, freedom to be as nasty as he wanted her to be. With his free hand, he dug his fingers into the flesh of her ass as he pulled her closer against his throbbing member. With a vicious growl, he brought his hand down sharply onto her ass, spanking her forcefully. She moaned loudly as he brought his hand down, again and again, keeping her pinned against him with his fist in her hair. The flesh of her buttocks stung more and more with every blow, and she could feel her pussy responding with an aching need, but she knew he wouldn't stop until her ass was bright red. She squirming against him as he spanked her, inching him closer and closer to her entrance, desperate to have him inside of her. He growled in her ear, bringing his hand even harder down onto her buttocks, knowing full well that it only made her want him all the more.

"You're so impatient, little one," he teased. "You just can't wait for Daddy to fuck you can you?" She whined and writhed against him, but he only spanked her again. His blows beginning to come harder and harder as he masterfully teased her, inflaming her desire.

"Tell Daddy what you want," he said. He loved to make her say the filthiest things, loved the way it only made her pussy wetter when she let herself be the depraved slut she tried to keep hidden away from the rest of the word. She knew that he would not give her what she so desperately needed until she asked for it, possibly even begged for it. She had gotten pretty good at begging these past few months, if she did say so herself.

"I want your cock, Daddy," she whined. "I want you to fuck me so hard that it hurts. Please give me your big fat cock, Daddy." Suddenly, he shifted her weight, flipping her onto her back and kneeling between her knees, pushing her legs wide open. She gasped loudly as he began to run the tip of his cock over her clit, rubbing it in slow circles. Nothing made him happier than torturing her with pleasure.

"Do you want Daddy's cock, is that it little one?" he said with a husky voice. She stared down, fascinated by the sight of his cock gliding over her, and nodded. "I didn't hear you that time, sweetie."

"Yes, I want your cock, Daddy. Please, I need it so bad, please fuck me!" With a satisfied sneer, he plunged into her, roaring with satisfaction as he buried himself inside of her to the hilt. Hannah made a roar of her own, grasping his buttocks to pull him closer. Her entire body felt alive as he stretched her open, taking her hard and fast. He unleashed his passion onto her, rutting into her like a crazed animal. His hands twisted into her hair, yanking her hair back as he drove himself into her furiously.

"Is that what you wanted, kitten?" he growled into her ear.

"Yes, Daddy. I love it when you fuck me

hard!" As his thick cock split her open again and again, she could feel a climax building. She raked her nails over his back and buttocks, wild with pleasure.

"Good girl," he laughed playfully. "Are you ready to cum for Daddy, princess?" He reached down and began to stroke her clit with his thumb as he pounded into her, overwhelming her with ecstasy. The double stimulation was too much for her, and she thrashed her head from side to side. If he didn't either stop or give her permission soon, she would totally lose control.

"Yes, Daddy. Can I please?" The effort of holding herself back made the words came out strangled.

"Yes, little one," he said, rubbing her clit even faster. "Cum for Daddy." Within seconds, another orgasm broke over her, stronger than the first. She let herself go completely, trembling and moaning beneath him.

"Oh fuck, baby girl, you're so tight around my cock." As Hannah's quaking orgasm began to recede, his thrusts quickened. She could feel his manhood grow even harder inside of her, throbbing on the edge of release. "Look at me." He loved maintaining eye contact as they fucked, loved to keep her attention focused solely on him. He yanked her hair harder to bring her face closer to his, holding her face firmly with his other hand. The possessive way his fingers dug into her face always gave her a sense of belonging.

"You're mine," he said, holding her gaze with his chocolate brown eyes. "Aren't you, slut? My slut." She never got tired of hearing it or saying it. She was his, and he was hers forever.

"I'm yours, Daddy," she whispered. He pulled her face to his for a kiss, deep but tender.

"Yes," he whispered, his breath hot against her lips. "All mine." His rhythm suddenly faltered, and she could feel his grip on her hair tightening as his body went rigid. His cock throbbed and twitched inside of her as he filled her up with his seed. With one final shudder, he collapsed against her and buried his face in her neck, his breath ragged. They didn't have the luxury of lingering in bed, however. Their morning sex usually didn't leave much time for breakfast, but it was well worth it in Hannah's mind. Even with the time crunch, he took the time to diaper her lovingly. She loved wearing her diaper all day at work. Not only did it provide her with a source of comfort when things got hectic, it also reminded her of Paul and what a truly wonderful Daddy he was to her. She loved being his little. They ate a quick breakfast together in contented silence, sipping coffee and reading the newspaper or their phones. Hannah treasured these quiet moments together before the hubbub of the day began. She loved her job and would be eternally grateful to Paul for helping her to land it, but it had its challenges and stresses just like any job. That hubbub began all too soon as she dumped her plate and cup in the sink and ran upstairs to get dressed. She mostly interacted with turtles and penguins all day, so she never wasted too much time on her hair and makeup. Most days, she just threw on some khaki shorts and the aquarium uniform and put her hair up in a ponytail.

"You look beautiful, baby girl," Paul said as she came back downstairs. He always said that, no matter how she looked, never letting her forget that she was his dream woman. She had expected his constant praise of her beauty to fade with time, but it hadn't. He still looked at her the same way as when they had first started dating. He was already dressed and had a travel mug of coffee for each of them ready to go.

"I love you so much, sweet girl," he said, kissing her sweetly and deeply. Even three months later, it always took her breath away, and she never got tired of hearing it.

"I love you too, Paul," she said. "I'll miss you today." As he kissed her again, she thought about their tentative discussions about consolidating their lives. Even though nothing had been decided yet, it felt to her more of a question of when rather than if. There would be a ton of details to work out such as who would move where, but it just made sense to simplify their lives by moving in together. They spent all of their time together anyway, so why not move in together? It just made sense. The two of them freely admitted that this was the happiest they had ever been. They both had jobs they loved nearby, and they fit together so well, supporting and loving each other unconditionally. Even when he had to go out of town for a work trip, she could usually get off of work from her own job to go with him. They rarely fought, facing any problem with honest, open communication. Hannah was never one to let bottled up feelings and mixed signals to ever threaten their happiness, and it turned out that Paul was the same way. As a result, this had been the healthiest and happiest relationship of her life, and she was determined to make it work for the long haul. Paul handed her a travel mug of coffee of her own, still groggily wiping the sleep from his eyes. He was not a morning person which made him getting up early enough to drive her to work all the more romantic.

"Are you ready to go, princess?" he asked, kissing her once more, this time on the forehead. Even though her car had been working just fine ever since they got it back from the mechanic, he still insisted on driving her to work and picking her up whenever their schedules allowed. He said it allowed them to spend more time together, something they always wanted more of. She was happy to oblige, happy to let him spoil and pamper her all he wanted. She freely admitted that he had spoiled her rotten as if either of them would have it any other way. No one else could ever come close to comparing with her Daddy.

"Yeah, I'm ready," she said. "Let's go." He kissed her softly, his lips lingering over hers, and sighed contentedly as he stared down at her with a quizzical expression on his face.

"Are you happy, my darling?" he asked. She grinned, certain that the answer was written all over her face.

"Completely."

Daddy's Assistant

A DDLG and ABDL erotic story about a Daddy Dom who trains his assistant to be his sexy baby girl

By Tina Moore

Chapter 1

Amber groaned as she tapped on her phone, calculating the final total for this month's bills, and put her head down despondently on the table.

"Is it really that bad?" Asked her roommate Leslie sympathetically. Amber only groaned again and nodded, pushing the phone in her direction. Leslie took a peek at the total on the calculator app on Amber's phone. It was enough to make even her wince. Not that Leslie was well off or anything, but she was at least steadily employed, which was more than Amber could say.

"Yikes. That's per person?" Leslie asked. Amber sighed and sat up. She scanned their threadbare apartment for anything she might be able to sell, but there was nothing left of any value. Handmade quilts gifted to you by your Aunt Betty weren't exactly top-ticket items, or so she had been told by several pawnshop owners. Everything else had been sold off already. It had been so long since she'd had any acting gig, much less a paying one, and all of her savings had dried up months ago.

"Yep," Amber replied as she downed the remainder of tea in her chipped mug and poured more hot water over the tea bag, steeping it for a second time. Pretty soon, she wouldn't be able to afford tea at all if things kept up this way.

"Sorry, hun," said Leslie.

"But that's going just about to wipe me out. I won't be able to loan you any more money this month," she added. Amber looked at her with guilt all over her face. It wasn't fair of her to keep borrowing money from her roommate, anyway. Leslie had problems of her own without Amber adding to them. She appreciated that Leslie had never tried to make her feel bad about not having enough money, but that didn't mean that it was ok for her to take advantage of that. She needed to figure out a more permanent solution.

"Fair enough. It's fine. I'll manage, don't worry about me. I have lots of plasma to sell," Amber replied.

"Look," Leslie sat down beside her at their small table, putting her hand over Amber's in a show of support.

"Why don't you get a temporary job?" Leslie offered.

"I know that I should, it's just that it feels so much like giving up. I came to the city to be an actress, not to be a waitress or gas attendant. I know I shouldn't expect to be famous overnight and that I have bills to pay. But at the same time, if I get a job, I might miss out on auditions. Also, I'm really a terrible waitress. I mean, just awful," Amber said with her head between her hands.

"I know, and that does suck but think of it like this. Would you really enjoy a summer of eating ramen and getting your plasma sucked out three times a week? How good would you really be in an audition with malnutrition and blood loss?" Leslie said. Amber managed a chuckle even as her shoulders sagged in defeat.

"No, I guess you're right. I'll hit up Craigslist, see what I can find," Amber said, sitting up. Leslie patted her hand consolingly and got up to retreat back to her spot in front of the television.

"Chin up. Maybe you can find something really chill," she said hopefully as she went to settle back down with her snacks. Amber hoped that she was right. Acting gigs were few and far between and seldom paid well. She had worked in retail and foodservice but found that she was far too anxious for that line of work. One angry word from a customer would rattle around in her head for days, and given her ineptitude in those areas, she heard a lot of angry words. Everything else that she had applied for had wanted years of experience that she didn't have, even the so-called entry-level positions. It was tough out there, no matter what line of work you were in. It would seem.

She opened her laptop and did a broad search,

quickly eliminating jobs that paid too little or had requirements that she didn't meet. One job, in particular, did look promising, however, a call for a personal assistant. *Seeking candidates with unusual levels of loyalty and devotion to their employer.* She pondered that for a moment, assuming they meant long hours with little pay. However, as she read through the advertisement, she noticed that the pay per hour listed was very impressive. There were very few details other than that to give her a clue as to what she might expect. Burning with curiosity, she replied to the email and attached her resume, then continued her search.

Nothing would probably come of it, she thought, *just like dozens of other applications that never get answered.* But if it did, she could certainly get used to that kind of money! She dreamed of paying Leslie back and saving enough money to once again rededicate herself to her craft. She cautioned herself against getting her hopes up but found herself dreaming about it anyway.

***

Malcolm sifted through a pile of resumes, bored with the task of finding a personal assistant for himself. This was the sort of thing that he used to delegate to Natasha before she had selfishly decided to abandon him.

You know that's not fair, he chided himself. Natasha had found the man of her dreams over the holidays, living right next door to her parents of all places, and decided to move halfway across the country to be with him. While Malcolm was happy for her if somewhat begrudgingly, it did leave him in a bit of a pickle, he doubted that he would find another assistant who was half as capable as Natasha had been. She was whip-smart, beautiful, and catered to his every whim, sexual and otherwise. Best of all, she followed his number one rule: don't fall in love. He preferred to keep things as professional as possible. He didn't have time for the messy emotional entanglements that come with dating and did not like the idea of hiring a prostitute, so he had found that striking up a certain arrangement with his personal assistants was the best course of action in that department.

It had taken a few false starts before he had found the perfect combination of competence and obedience in Natasha, and he loathed the thought of having to go through the process all over again. What were the chances of finding another Natasha? Truly that girl had been one in a million. Wearily, he checked his messages and to his surprise, saw a rather promising email in response to his online ad. He quickly looked the candidate up on social media and saw that she was pretty, young, and almost heartbreakingly naive looking. He could feel himself respond to her picture immediately, blood rushing to his cock as soon as he saw her smile, wide and innocent. This one would be worth meeting, certainly. She would look so sexy kneeling before him with only a diaper on and a collar around her neck. He typed out a quick reply, specifying the time and place that he expected her to meet him, already dreaming of keeping her under his desk to pleasure him any time he wanted. Her innocent smile made him want to corrupt her to make her his completely. It had only been a few days since Natasha moved out, and already his sex drive was through the roof. He checked the application again and saw that this new girl's name was Amber. He closed his eyes and thought about tying up sweet Amber, forcing orgasm after orgasm onto her helpless body until she was a drooling, babbling mess. He could tell just by looking at her that this one would require quite a bit of training, which he very much looked forward to giving it to her.

He pulled his cock out, stroking it fiercely as he imagined throat training her. He would keep her in a diaper and collar, nothing else, as he taught her how to deepthroat him. He didn't mind admitting that he had a huge cock, and most women struggled when it came to giving him head. When he got through with sweet, little Amber, however, she would swallow him down like the well-trained whore he hoped her to become. He ached to fondle her perfect perky breasts as she choked on him, taking every inch of him down her bulging throat. A ragged sigh escaped his lips as he furiously jerked himself, enjoying the mental image. She almost certainly had never had a Daddy, and he looked forward to showing her all of the fun that could be had. She would look so cute begging for his cum, begging him to fuck her. Most of all, she would look so cute cumming all over his cock. He wanted to make all of her worries melt away, to her the luxury of thinking only about surrendering to his pleasure. As he thought of making her his princess, he erupted jizz all over his hands and pants, wishing it was filling up Amber's tight little pussy instead. She would be his, he vowed. She would be his very soon.

Chapter 2

Amber ran down the sidewalk breathlessly, clutching a scrap of paper that had the correct time and address hurriedly scrawled on it. She couldn't afford a cab ride across town, and so she decided to leave early enough to walk. It was a very long walk, taking her hours. Somewhere along the way, she had gotten a bit lost, however, and was having to really hustle to make it on time. At last, she found the correct building number, confirming with the doorman that Mr. Graham did, in fact, live there. She breathed a sigh of relief, as it looked as though she would actually make it on time, even if just barely. Once inside the elevator, she punched in the floor and the security code he had given her. To her surprise, the elevator opened up to a living space. She stepped forward tentatively into the nicest apartment she had ever seen, peeking around the corners to see if she saw anyone.

"Hello?" she called out but didn't hear a response. She stepped further into the room and craned her neck to peek up the stairs. She heard noises, so she stepped onto the bottom stair, trying to get close enough to hear what was going on without intruding.

"Oh, Daddy," she heard a female voice saying.

"Yeah, fuck me with that big dick, Daddy!" Came the voice, making Amber's eyes go wide. Amber gasped and felt her face growing hot. She ran back toward the elevator, not sure what she should do. Her instinct was to run away and hide, feeling like she had violated someone's privacy somehow. But, as she reached out for the elevator button, she stopped herself. She was at the correct location at the correct time. The security code wouldn't have worked if she had punched in the wrong floor by mistake. If she had interrupted something, that was hardly her fault. She smoothed her hair and skirt to compose herself once more and sat on the couch, as far away from the stairs as physically possible, and decided to wait as long as it took. She tried to tune out the sex noises, but they certainly weren't making it easy. She heard moans and loud smacks and a steady thumping. As it seemed to go on and on, she found herself getting a little heated herself.

Wildly inappropriate, she chided herself. Still, it seemed as though the two of them were having a marvelous time, and she found herself to be a little jealous. It had been quite some time since she had been on a date. Trying to be an actress took up so much of her time and energy that it didn't leave much room for anything else. Even when she had had sex last, it wasn't nearly as much fun as whatever these two were getting up to. The guy, Greg she thought his name was, had been very nice but very boring. He didn't exactly make her see fireworks, and she never retook his calls. At last, the two seemed to finish up, their climatic moans echoing throughout the entire apartment. Amber cleared her throat and straightened her blazer, trying her best to ignore the heat between her legs.

Ten minutes later, a woman descended the stairs, a young brunette in a pants suit similar to Amber's. She nodded politely to Amber on her way out but otherwise didn't acknowledge her. The woman got on the elevator and left, and still, Amber waited. She was on the verge of leaving when, at last, a man in a pair of black slacks and a crisp, white shirt came down the stairs. He was easily the most handsome man she had ever seen, with dark hair, dark eyes, and five o'clock shadow sprinkled over a rugged jawline. He spotted her on the couch and didn't say anything for a moment, only put his hands in his pockets and looked her up and down appraisingly. The way that he assessed her was strangely arousing to her, something in the way that his eyes appeared hungry yet cold at the same time. She did her best not to flinch or blush but rather to meet his penetrating gaze with one of her own. Despite the fluttering in her stomach, she somehow succeeded.

"Ms. Bennet, you're early," he said at last. His voice was low and gravelly, sending pleasant tingles all through her. Despite his arrogant attitude, she found herself drawn to him. He had a dominance, a sort of gravitas about him, that she had never experienced before.

"I was exactly on time, actually," she corrected. Again, they just stared at each other, matching stoney gaze for stoney gaze. She was surprised by her own boldness. Normally, she wasn't one to challenge authority figures. But then, most authority figures didn't ignite some strange passion inside of her that she didn't fully understand. All that heat had to go somewhere, she supposed.

"Come," he said after studying her for a long moment and began to walk away without so much as looking back to see if she followed. She suppressed an eye roll at his continued rudeness and followed him to his office. As he poured himself a drink at the minibar, she sat in a chair opposite his desk and waited patiently.

"Would you care for a drink?" he asked.

"It's ten-thirty in the morning," she responded, careful to keep her tone even. He snapped his head around and glared at her anyway.

"I didn't ask you what time it is. I asked you if you wanted a drink." His tone was low and vaguely threatening, but she didn't let that rattle her. Or at least, it didn't intimidate her so much as it heightened her attraction to him. She found his dominant energy to be refreshingly stimulating. She was surprised at her own reaction, but it was so strong that it was impossible to fight it or deny it.

"No, thank you," she said, still keeping her tone polite. He sat down at his desk and took a sip of his drink before speaking.

"Ms. Bennet, I should start by saying that this is not your normal personal assistant position. I want to be very upfront about that. If it makes you uncomfortable or you don't think you can handle it, we will end this interview right now, no questions asked. If you believe that you can and want to fulfill my expectations, then we can proceed. Do you understand?" The handsome stranger asked.

"I understand. What exactly are these unusual expectations you speak of?" She replied nodding her head.

"First of all, I will require you to live here full time. I am a demanding employer, and I expect you to be at my beck and call twenty-four-seven. Secondly, I will require you to service me in every way possible." He leaned forward, watching her reaction closely, letting the words hang in the air. She picked up on the insinuation immediately but didn't react right away, not even so much as a raised eyebrow. She knew that she should be disgusted, that she should get her purse and leave in an indignant huff. She played the scene in her head, imagined the cutting words she would say, putting him in his place as she left him to wallow in his own lechery. She knew that's what she should do, but the curious tingle between her legs kept her in her chair and under his penetrating stare. She found that she didn't want to put him in his place but rather the other way around.

"You understand what I'm referring to, of course," he prompted when she didn't say anything for a while. She nodded slowly, feeling as if he had put her under some sort of trance or spell. She didn't understand where these thoughts or urges were coming from.

"Good," he purred. "I am a man of unusual tastes, and I require my partner to do whatever I say, whenever I say it, without question. This is true both in business and in the bedroom." Again, the alarm bells that were telling her to get out of there were far outweighed by the clenching heat she felt within her core as she thought about being under his command. Her breath quickened slightly, and she felt almost drunk. She swallowed, finding her voice at last.

"Your girlfriend doesn't object to this arrangement?" She was still somehow managing to keep an even tone of voice, as though they were having a perfectly normal conversation as if this were a perfectly normal job interview.

"I don't have a girlfriend. If you are referring to the young lady who just left, she is another candidate for the position. She was eager to show just how obedient she could be and wanted to audition. Don't worry about her, though. She wasn't up for some of my more unusual requests. I don't think I'll be hearing from her again." She swallowed hard, wondering what the deal-breaker had been and if she would be able to handle it any better. There was no way to know but to try, after all. She found that she was eager to prove herself to him. Even though she had just met him, she found herself wanting to make him proud.

"Will you be required me to ... audition as well?" she asked, almost afraid of the answer. Her eagerness was mixed with more than a little nervousness. This was all so new.

"Only if you want to, but I do not require it. I have a good feeling about you, Amber. You seem," he paused, taking in a deep breath as he looked her up and down again, his gaze lingering on her breasts. "Different. I believe you and I are going to get along quite well. However, why don't we each take the evening to think it over and touch base tomorrow? We wouldn't want to be too hasty, now would we?"

"Alright," she heard herself say distantly. Every time he gave her one of those intense looks, it turned her brain to jelly, and it became impossible to think straight. Perhaps it was wise to sleep on it. She stood on shaky legs and extended her hand to shake. He took it, rubbing his thumb over her palm, making her gasp quietly as a jolt of electric desire gripped her. He smiled arrogantly, almost a sneer. On any other man, it would have been offputting, but on him, it was a powerful aphrodisiac.

"Until we meet again," he said and kissed the back of her hand, holding her gaze as he did so. She nodded at him politely and left the room, unable to ignore the fact that her panties were soaking wet. She reserved the right to change her mind once her hormones had settled down, of course, but right then, she was leaning heavily towards a yes. The idea of giving her body over to this man was the most exciting thing to happen to her in quite some time.

Chapter 3

Amber found it almost impossible to sleep that evening, her conversation with Mr. Graham kept running over and over in her mind. As much as she knew she should reject his offer outright, she found that she actually wanted to accept it, even after his intoxicating influence had worn off. Something about him fascinated her, made her crave to be around him, to be his. Even his vague references to his dark desires left her both curious and titillated. The woman who had interviewed before her had been joyfully calling him Daddy, which was shocking enough to Amber's inexperienced sensibilities. Her mind raced as she wondered what it could have been that scared her off. She couldn't stop imagining fucking Mr. Graham, calling him Daddy in her mind as he pounded into her. Instead of being turned off by the taboo, she found it incredibly arousing and started rubbing herself over the top of her pajama pants. In her mind's eye, she saw his penetrating gaze, staring into her eyes as he held her down, pinning her wrists down over her head with his strong hands. She wondered what it would feel like to have him inside of her, to let him use her body however he wished like some kind of erotic plaything. It sounded so vulgar, and yet it made her so wet.

She slipped her hand under the waistband and started rubbing her clit frantically, shuddering as the pleasure intensified. "You're mine," she heard him say in her mind as he took her savagely. She found that she craved to belong to him, to serve him. It made her pussy throb to think of herself as being under his control. She pinched her nipples as she thought of his commanding energy and dominant tone of voice. Sometimes, late at night, she had fantasized about being someone's sexual plaything just as she was now, and only this time, there was a chance that it could actually become a reality. She wondered if he would keep her in chains or in some sort of elaborate sex dungeon. The thought of being bound and spread before him made her cum. Biting her lip to muffle her soft noises of pleasure, she quivered under her covers and then finally quieted, gasping and limp-bodied. In the cold light of the next morning, however, she once again doubted whether it was a good idea. If she was concerned about a part-time job not leaving her with enough time for acting, how would being a live-in personal assistant be any better?

On the other hand, the pay was so good she would be able to save money, especially if she sublet her room while she was working for him. Within a few months, she would have enough saved enough that she could focus only on acting for a while. As she was thinking it over, she heard her phone buzz.

I have decided that you will begin working for me tomorrow. A driver will arrive at your place at 9 AM sharp. Do not be late. Respond "Yes, Daddy" if you agree. Even in his texts, he was commanding.

She felt a surge of desire for him and knew that there was no way that she could turn down this opportunity.

Yes, Daddy. She smiled as she typed the words, already looking forward to her new life.

***

Amber spent the rest of the day packing her things. She explained to Leslie that her new job required her to be on call day and night. She decided that leaving out the more sordid details was probably prudent. Luckily, Leslie said that she knew of a co-worker who was hunting for a new place, and before the day was done, all of the details had been ironed out. Amber would move out tomorrow, and the new girl would move in the following day and take over her portion of the rent and utilities from that point on until further notice. Amber would leave her furniture behind for the other girl to use so she wouldn't have to rent a storage unit and only take her personal items with her to

Malcolm's. That evening, Amber found it difficult to sleep. She was so excited and nervous that not even masturbating could soothe her to sleep. Even after she made herself cum, she still ached for her new Daddy, as she was already calling him in her mind. Her mind raced as she tried to imagine what sort of kinky things he would want to do to her which only made her horny all over again. After a fitful night of tossing and turning, it was finally time to go to him.

She was waiting for the driver when he arrived, suspecting that he would not hesitate to tattle on her if she kept him waiting. What little she knew about Malcolm so far made her assume that he was going to be a very strict boss. The driver put her bags in the trunk and told her to help herself to any of the drinks or snacks, but Amber found that she was too nervous to eat and could not bring herself to pour a drink at nine in the morning even if it would calm her down. Funny how selling herself to a perfect stranger didn't make her blink an eye, but day drinking was a bridge too far. She stifled a giggled and shrugged at her own quirkiness. As they arrived at Mr. Graham's building, her bags were passed off to the doorman, who escorted her into the elevator as though she were some terribly important person. When the door opened again, Mr. Graham was waiting for them, again wearing perfectly tailored black slacks. His button-up was navy blue today, setting off his chocolate brown eyes perfectly. Just the mere sight of him instantly made Amber's body grow hot with desire. Without a word, he slipped the doorman some cash and took Amber's bags from him.

"Come," he said once they were alone again. "I will show you to your room." He led her up the stairs where she saw that his apartment was even larger than she had imagined. The room he had put aside for her was luxurious with a four-poster bed, a dresser, and vanity, even a gorgeous cherry wood bookcase filled with books of all sorts. She couldn't wait to get her hands on those books and hoped that she would have time to read as his assistant.

Mr. Graham put her bags on the floor and turned to face her. There was none of the coldness in his eyes that had been present at their first meeting. Now there was only pure, raw hunger as he looked her up and down. All thoughts left her mind as the air between them grew thick with electricity.

"From this moment on, you are mine. You will submit to me in every way. Is that understood?" She suppressed a shiver of excitement as his words filled her with a jolt of electric heat. It was unbelievable how aroused she had gotten just from that one sentence. He locked his eyes onto hers, and she was filled with a need to please him, to obey him. Slowly, she nodded her head.

"I'm afraid that's not good enough, sweet little Amber. I need to hear you say it, to make sure that you truly understand what I am asking of you." He stepped closer to her as he spoke, dominant confidence rolling off of him in waves, heightening her excitement and leaving her feeling more than a little dazed with lust.

"From this moment," she repeated dutifully. "I am yours. I will submit to you in every way." He smiled and stroked her face with the back of his hand. Surprised by the soft gesture, she let her eyes flutter closed for a moment, before opening them to find he was staring at her with an intensity that made her legs feel weak. The way he looked at made her feel like he could see directly into her mind.

"From now on, you will call me Daddy at all times." He was so close that his warm breath washed over her lips as he spoke. She yearned for him to close that distance and put his lips on hers, but she knew what he expected of her and knew that she must perform her duty.

"Yes, Daddy," she whispered, leaning into his heat with the hope that he would reward her good behavior with a kiss.

"Good," he said curtly and stepped back, breaking the spell. Her body cried out for him, but he quickly returned to a business-like manner, and the moment passed. "We have a lot of work to do today. The first order of business is to solidify our contract."

"Contract?" she asked, somewhat confused. He chuckled affectionately at the dumbfounded look on her face that was also mixed with a pouting disappointment.

"Yes, little one. It is vital that we both protect ourselves, legally speaking. I will allow you twenty minutes to unpack your things, and then you will meet me in my office downstairs. Is that clear?"

"Yes, Daddy," she said automatically, already allowing herself to slip into a submissive state of mind. It already felt so natural, as though she could deny him nothing.

"Good girl,' he said, making her body feel hotter, her need growing so intense that her body cried out for his touch. To her great disappointment, he only kissed her forehead lightly before leaving the room abruptly. She sat on the bed, her head spinning. That gentle gesture of kissing her on the forehead did not at all line up with his otherwise harsh demeanor, and it left her completely disoriented, wondering if she fully understood what was happening here after all. Suddenly, having everything written out in black and white seemed like a very good idea.

Chapter 4

She joined him downstairs at the specified time. It hadn't taken her long to unpack her things, and she had spent the rest of the time perusing the bookshelf, trying to decide which one she wanted to read first. When she came into his office, he already had a copy of the contract out on the desk ready for her to read. The contract was surprisingly vague, only covering legal liability while leaving her to wonder at the day-to-day specifics, much as she had done for days now. He explained all of the legalese to her patiently and put the whole thing in layman's terms. Basically, both parties were free to end the arrangement at any time with no questions asked, and both parties were barred from discussing any of the specifics with anyone else to protect their privacy. It did, however, provide her with a generous severance package should either of them decide that they wanted to end things, which surprised her. Nothing in the contract alarmed her, so Amber signed it right away, eager to get on with it. He slipped it into an envelope and placed it in his desk drawer.

"Now," he said matter of factly. "It is time to show you where you will be staying during your training period." Her brow wrinkled in confusion.

"I won't be staying in my room?" He leaned back in his chair, tenting his hands and staring at her for a moment. She knew that he was only doing it to make her squirm, but that didn't stop it from working. She longed to know what he was thinking when he looked at her that way: something filthy, no doubt.

"No," he said, once he had made her sufficiently uncomfortable. "You will have to earn that privilege. Follow me." With no further explanation, he took her back upstairs and led her to a room next to her bedroom. He stood by the door and gestured toward the handle.

"Go on," he prompted. With a shaky hand, she reached forward and opened the door slowly, her heart pounding with nervous anticipation. On the other side was a nursery or so it seemed. Upon closer inspection, however, it seemed that everything was adult-sized. The crib was as big as a twin-sized bed, and the changing station was enormous, big enough to comfortably fit a grown-up. She looked around at the sea of pastels and stuffed animals, more confused than ever. This was nothing like what she had expected to find. Still not explained, he went to the closet and opened it to reveal a long row of frilly dresses, choosing a light purple one from the rack. He lay the garment down on the changing table and pulled out an adult diaper from the built-in drawer, laying it on top of the dress. She couldn't tear her eyes away from the diaper. Surely he didn't expect her to wear one of those.

"Strip," he said commandingly. She blinked at him, flabbergasted.

"But - "

"Little girls don't argue," he said firmly. "Little girls do as they are told. Strip. I want to see what is mine." Something in his tone of voice stopped all of her objections in their tracks. Before she even knew what she was doing, she was lifting her shirt over her head. She began to hurriedly slide her skirt to the floor, but he stopped her with a gesture.

"Slower," he said, his eyes burning into her. Matching his stare, she let her hands slide down over the curves of her hips before peeling her skirt down slowly. He made a quiet noise of approval as the garment hit the floor, leaving her only in her underwear. He smirked as she undid the clasp of her bra, holding it place with her hands for a moment as she let the straps dangle, teasing him. As she let it drop to the floor along with her skirt, revealing her perky breasts, he drew a sharp breath, and the bulge in his pants grew more obvious. Lastly, she slid her panties down, showing him her freshly shaved pussy.

"That's better. Good girl," he purred as she

stood before him completely naked. "You are a very sexy young lady. For the duration of your training period, you will wear neither a bra nor panties. Only diapers and dresses from now on, is that understood?"

"Yes, Daddy," she said, feeling small and vulnerable. While she didn't fully understand, she found that her eagerness to serve outweighed her need to understand. He began to move towards her, slowly like a predatory cat who has spotted its prey. Holding her in his gaze, he reached out and casually stroked her breast, pinching her nipple lightly between his fingers. Her breath caught at the sensation of aching need that suddenly gripped her. He moved closer to her, close enough to kiss her, but again, he refrained. He lifted her up by her hips and put her on the changing table. She loved the way it felt to be handled by him, the way he lifted her up as though she weighed nothing. It made her feel like a delicate doll.

"Lay back," he instructed and positioned the diaper underneath her. With a practiced hand, he had the diaper in place and had it fastened within seconds.

"Up," he commanded and had her sit with her arms above her head so that he could put the dress on her. Once she was properly zipped up, he picked her up again and placed her back on her feet.

"Turn around," he said. "Slowly." She did a slow spin, mindful of his eyes on her as she let him look at her from every angle. He nodded in approval and bent down to retrieve something from another drawer.

"You look beautiful, princess, but there is just one thing missing." It was a box in his hand, and when he opened it, there was a pacifier inside. He took it from the box and laid it gently in her mouth.

"There. Now you are absolutely perfect."mHe kissed the handle of her pacifier, and she blushed.

Chapter 5

She had expected him to fuck her there and then, but he didn't. He took her downstairs to his office and gave her a brief overview of the business side of their relationship. He was a lawyer who worked primarily from home, but, as he explained, he would occasionally have to go into the office, much more rarely, so would she. He had a paralegal and a secretary for most of the things directly related to his law practice, he said. Most of what she would be doing was attending to his personal needs: errands, housework, scheduling, that kind of thing. Her mind was racing, but every time she started to ask a question, he put up a hand to stop her.

"Don't you worry your pretty little head about that right now. For the duration of your training period, you will not be expected to do anything other than learning how to be a perfect little girl for Daddy. That is your primary job until further notice," Her mind burned with further questions, but he only pushed to pacifier back in her mouth, effectively cutting off any further conversation. He made her lunch, making her sit in a highchair as she ate. She was sort of taken aback by that if anything she assumed she would be responsible for making their meals. He wouldn't even let her eat by herself, insisting on feeding her bite by bite. Everything was happening so quickly, and none of it was as she had expected it to be. None of it was unpleasant so far, just unexpected. He declared that after lunch, she would have to take a nap and she found herself to actually be grateful for the break. There was so much to process, and it was making her feel drained, even a little anxious. He carried her to the nursery and sat in a rocking chair with her in his lap. His arms engulfed her, warm and strong, and she found herself melting into him. He stroked her hair as he rocked her, and the comforting sensations soothed her frayed nerves. It felt so nice to forget about her questions and just let herself be babied for a while. The lack of sleep from the night before combined with the stress of the day caught up with her as she rested in his arms and she began to nod off. Despite how much she needed the rest, she found herself fighting it a little, not wanting to leave the bliss and safety of his arms, even for the sweet respite of sleep. Eventually, however, she gave in, and her heavy lids closed. He lifted her, slowly and gently, and she was just awake enough to register that he laid her down in the crib, covered her with a blanket, and kissed her on the forehead.

"Sleep tight, baby girl," he whispered and tiptoed out of the room.

***

When she awoke from her nap, she felt refreshed and energized. She sat up to see that the crib had her essentially locked in. She could get out if she really needed to in an emergency, but for the most part, she was stuck. As she stretched and wiped the sleep from her eyes, she noticed that she had to use the bathroom. She looked around the room, spotting a baby monitor on the dresser.

"Daddy?" she called out tentatively, not sure if the thing was even on. Sure enough, he came into the room just a few moments later.

"Well, hello, princess," he said fondly as he approached the crib. "Did you have a nice nap?"

"Yes, it was nice, thank you. I need to go to the bathroom, can you let me out?" He shook his head.

"No. You can get out of your crib if you want, but potties are for big girls. Little girls use their diapers." She froze and stared at him, not sure if she had heard him correctly. Did he really expect her to pee herself? Wearing a diaper was one thing; she was happy to play along if that pleased him in some way. But the thought of wetting herself made her burn with embarrassment.

"What? What do you mean?" She hoped

beyond hope that she had misunderstood, that there was some other explanation.

"Exactly what I said, little one. You go potty in your diaper from now on. Are you going to do what Daddy says, or am I going to have to spank you?" She could tell that from the tone in his voice that it wouldn't be the kind of playful, sexy spanking that she heard people talk about from time to time. She had a feeling that he would make sure that she wouldn't like the spanking that he gave her one little bit. She squirmed, the need to urinate only growing stronger. The last thing she wanted was to screw this up on her very first day. Even more than that, she didn't want to disappoint him.

"Ok, Daddy," she said. "I'll try." Try as she might, however, not a drop would come out. She seemed to have some sort of mental block against it. Her heart plummeted as he scowled at her, his anger feeling like the most devastating thing in the world. She could feel the tears begin to spring to her eyes, blurring her vision. "I- I can't ..." He looked at her with a strange combination of emotions on his face. He looked like he was about to say something, but didn't. As he finally started to move toward her, she flinched away from him.

"There, there, little one," he said, putting a comforting hand on her shoulder. "Daddy isn't angry. I know you tried. This is for your own good, to help you learn and grow. Understand?" She didn't really understand, but she knew that he didn't want her to be afraid, so she sniffled and nodded anyway, putting on a brave face. He took her hand and led her to the bed, where he sat. He suddenly seemed much more imposing to her, as if he had grown a few inches in the last few seconds but she knew that was only a result of her fear and shame.

"Over my lap," he said firmly but gently. Her eyes were still streaming with tears, but she complied, laying herself over his firm thighs. It was uncomfortable to have the full weight of her body pressing on her overfull bladder and made the urge to go that much more intense. He lifted her skirt and several moments passed in silence. The anticipation grew, and she felt that was almost worse than the spanking itself would be. Just as she was about to turn to look at him, he brought his hand down hard on her butt. It didn't hurt very much, not at first, as the padding of the diaper dampened the blows somewhat. As he continued to spank her, however, the pain grew in intensity. She began to squirm to get away, but his firm hand around her waist kept her locked in place. The pain and humiliation began to mount, and Amber kicked her legs futilely.

To make matters worse, she could feel the heat between her legs that told her that she liked what he was doing to her, despite the embarrassment and pain. Or possibly because of it. The thought only made her cry harder as shame and desire made her whole body tremble.

"You need to learn to obey Daddy," he explained calmly. He methodically covered every square inch of her bottom without mercy. The blows growing faster and harder as he went. She began to wail as the onslaught continued and she soon found herself so overwhelmed with emotion and sensation that her bladder simply released itself. It was a relief physically, but also mentally, a huge wave of satisfaction washed over her as she knew that Daddy would be pleased with her once again.

"I peed," she cried out, sobbing with relief. The spanking stopped at last, and Malcolm scooped her up into his arms, holding her close. She sank against his warm chest in relief and let the rest of her sobs peter out slowly as he held her, rocking her back and forth soothingly as she cried. All of the fear and embarrassment came flooding out of her along with her tears, along with a multitude of unidentifiable emotions that had built up over time. She let it all out, feeling completely safe and supported in his arms.

"There, isn't that better?" he murmured against her hair as he sobs began to slow down. She gripped her arms around his neck and nodded, noticing how not only did her bladder feel better, but she felt oddly cleansed after having such an intense cry. Now, with his arms around her, keeping her safe, she felt more open and free. She sighed happily, letting herself relax completely in his embrace. She even enjoyed the warm puffiness between her legs, still glowing with pride at her accomplishment. After a long time, he began to pat and squeeze the now puffy diaper. She was sure that she felt a bulge in his pants as he touched her and it was a relief to know that she wasn't the only one who had gotten turned on.

"Ready to get cleaned up, little one?" he asked. Again, she nodded, feeling a bit shy suddenly. At first, the wetness in her diaper had been warm and pleasant, but now she found herself wanting to be rid of the stickiness between her legs. He picked her up and carried her to the changing table.

"Daddy is so very proud of you, baby girl. You did such a good job of using your diaper, and you took your spanking so well. It will get easier to use your diaper, and before you know it, you'll love it, you'll see." He took the old, soggy diaper off, bundling it up and throwing it away. His praise and reassurance made her glow with pride. He began to clean her up. The baby wipe was soft and sensual against her pussy. Malcolm took his time, lovingly caressing her with the wipe, his breath obviously quickening as he did so. It was having an effect on her as well; the hungry look on his face igniting the desire that had begun to kindle when he spanked her. Again, she expected him to want to fuck her then or make some kind of move in that direction at least, but instead, he only replaced her diaper with a clean one and let her down again.

"Daddy has to get some work done in his office. Think you'll be ok on your own for a little while?"

"Yes, Daddy," she said. It was amazing to her how a single day of this lifestyle had already made her feel so regressed. She did feel a little nervous about being by herself for a while, strangely enough, but she was determined to put on a brave face for Daddy. Already, making him proud seemed like the most important thing in the world to her.

"I have some toys and coloring books for you to play with," he said, showing her the toy box and the little bookshelf with coloring books.

"Can I watch TV?" she asked hopefully, but he shook his head.

"Not now, little one. You can watch some cartoons before bed tonight if you are a good girl." She pouted slightly but nodded anyway, knowing that it would be futile to argue. Her still sore bottom reminded her to be on her best behavior. She crouched down to examine the toys more closely, her face lighting up when she discovered a race car track with a dozen or so cars to race.

"Have fun, baby girl," he said, watching her become engrossed with constructing the track for a moment before going back to his office, closing the door behind him.

Chapter 6

He came back sometime later to announce that dinner was ready. As he opened the door, the scent of chicken and herbs wafted into the room, and Amber's stomach suddenly growled. She had been so lost in her playtime that she hadn't even noticed how much time had passed or that she was hungry. Again, he fed her in the highchair, cutting her food up for her and feeding it to her one bite at a time. Already, her regression was beginning to feel normal. She was growing used to being fed and changed and had even enjoyed her playtime without feeling self-conscious about it. As he fed her, she couldn't help but wonder if those tendencies had been there all along or if her desire for him, her need to please him, was what made those activities so enjoyable for her. When they had finished eating, Malcolm cleaned up quickly and then announced that it was bath time. He carried her to the bathroom and turned on the water, sprinkling in some bubbles to make the bath nice and foamy. There were some bath time toys, rubber duckies, and plastic tugboats and the like along the rim of the tub that she looked forward to playing with.

"Arms up," he commanded and lifted her dress over her head. He took a moment to admire her semi-naked form, her smooth skin, and perky breasts. As his eyes moved over her, she could feel a familiar heat rising in her face and a tingle between her legs, the hunger in his face making her feel both flustered and aroused. "You are so beautiful, baby girl. So perfect." He took her diaper off next, tossing it in the trash, and ran his hands lightly over her skin, exploring her stomach, hips, and buttocks with his fingertips. His light touch raised goosebumps on her skin, and she could feel herself getting wet as he let his hands wander lower, grazing over her inner thighs and the outside of her sex. She gasped softly as he dipped a finger into her folds quickly, smirking as he found the wetness pooled there. He raised a finger to his lips, keeping her gaze locked with his as he tasted her juices.

"Oh, baby girl, whatever has gotten you so wet?" he teased. He stepped closer to her, placing his hands on either side of her face, kissing her lightly on the lips. She leaned in for more, but he pulled back, picking her up to lower her into the tub, which was now full of water and bubbles. He took a loofah and scrubbed her entire body lovingly and thoroughly. It felt so wonderful to be pampered. She couldn't recall the last time she had been the object of such intense focus, much less from such a handsome man. The warm water was so relaxing while his touch was both soothing and stirring. She surrendered to the sensations, letting herself go as he lavished her with attention. She was so zoned out that it almost felt like no time had passed before he was rinsing her off and draining the tub. He lifted her up and wrapped her in a towel, cradling her to his chest. He didn't seem to mind that she was getting his shirt wet with her still dripping wet hair. He sat on the rim of the tub and held her for a long time, kissing the top of her head as she slowly dripped dry. He held her so tightly that she found it hard to believe that she had only known this man for a little more than a day. He certainly seemed to be a man of great passion and deep emotion, based on the time they had spent together so far. She had been expecting a great deal of kinky sex, but cuddles and loving bubble baths were a surprise.

A very welcome surprise, she thought, burrowing her face further into his chest. It may have been a surprise, but it turned out to be exactly what she needed. Eventually, he rose and carried her to her nursery, laying her down on the crib. He brought out a pink frilly nightgown from the dresser and a fresh diaper. After he had dressed her, he began combing out her hair, delicately unsnarling the knots.

"So, after a full day of living here, what do you think? Would you like to continue?" he asked, his voice low and velvety. It was the first time he had spoken to her as an adult all day, and she found it was a bit difficult to shift gears and it took her a moment to find her words.

"Yes, Daddy," she said. "It isn't exactly what I expected, but I like it here." He smiled and patted her head. He looked so nice when he smiled, she noticed.

"Let me guess, you thought we would be fucking by now?" he teased. She found herself blushing but nodded, admitting that it was true. "Not to brag, but if it were just about sex, I wouldn't need to hire someone. You are here to fulfill all of my needs, little one, and that goes far beyond just the simple act of intercourse. We will get around to that when the time is right, of course. In the meantime, I have a need to nurture, to protect. I need someone in my life who belongs to me completely, who will give me not only their body but their obedience as well. Being a Daddy is just who I am, and I can't keep that confined to just the bedroom. That's why I enter into these arrangements. Does that make a little more sense, baby girl?" She nodded and smiled at him, happy to have that little glimpse into his inner thoughts.

"Now, that's enough grown-up talk. Ready for bed, little one?" She rubbed her eyes, feeling a bit tired but not ready to end the day yet.

"Almost," she said. He laughed and took the hint.

"Alright, I will read you one book before bedtime. Deal?"

"Deal!" she said gleefully. He tucked her in and brought her a selection of stuffies to sleep with. Before it was all said and done, he ended up reading her two and a half books before she nodded off to sleep. They were relatively short books, appropriate for her regressed state of mind, and her excitement kept her from drifting off. Finally, her breaths grew long and even, and he let himself out as quietly as possible.

Chapter 7

Malcolm closed the door behind him, letting out a huge breath that he didn't realize that he had been holding. As he walked the short distance down the hall to his bedroom, he began to chide himself for his foolish behavior. In every contract that he had ever signed with a little, he had always included one important rule: do not fall in love. But for some reason, when he was writing up the contract with Amber, he couldn't bring himself to include it this time. He couldn't place what it was exactly; after all, they had only met for that initial interview at the time that he was drawing it up. Even then, he could already tell there was something special about her, some little voice in his head telling him that if he put in that clause, he would live to regret it. As he spent the day with her, he began to be able to pinpoint what it was that had him so ensorcelled. She was sweet, naturally submissive and eager to please. Contrastingly, she also seemed to have a dirty side to her that responded well to his dominance over her. The combination was intoxicating, and he feared that he was in danger of falling for this one.

Would that be such a bad thing, he found himself wondering. The bachelor lifestyle was beginning to lose its charms. He had to admit. For so long, he had told himself that he didn't have time for the complications of romance. There was nothing complicated about the way Amber made him feel, however. She was a joy to be around, and he could already feel his disposition improving after one day with her. It felt good to have someone to take care of again, especially someone so sweet. He quickly pushed the thought out of his head, telling himself that he was getting all excited over nothing. They had only just met, no need to get himself all worked up over something that could potentially fizzle out within the week. Just in case it didn't, he did have to admit that he was glad that he had left out the love clause. If she did stick around, there was no way he would be able to adhere to it. Still, she had a grip over his thoughts as few women ever had before. He thought about her sexy body and how cute and innocent she looked when she was only wearing her diaper. He thought about how wet her pussy had gotten just from being naked in front of him, how the very act of making him happy seemed to turn her on. It was his preference not to have sex with his submissives until he was satisfied with their regression and submission to him in every way, but he could tell already that this one was going to be a challenge.

He stripped all of his clothes off and fell back on the bed, already stroking his hard cock before his head hit the pillow. Thoughts of Amber haunted him, and it was all the more painful because she was only a couple of doors away. Worse still, he knew that she was every bit as hungry for him as he was for her. He thought of sneaking into her room while she slept and climbing into bed with her, stopping her sleepy questions with a deep kiss. He longed to rip all of her clothing off and plunge himself into her, to feel her tight pussy gripping him. He imagined her moaning and thrashing with pleasure underneath him, her legs wrapped around him with all of her fierce little strength. He saw himself ramming into her without mercy, making sure that she felt how badly he wanted her with every thrust. All of the sexual tension that had been building came rushing out of him as he imagined what that would feel like and he found himself climaxing much sooner than he usually did. As he came, he imagined filling her tight pussy up with his seed, and he shuddered with ecstasy at the thought, wanting so much to feel it dripping out around him. Once he regained his breath, he began to clean himself up. It was going to be difficult to hold back, but he told himself that the waiting would make it all the sweeter once he finally gave in and claimed her. He wasn't willing to spoil the whole thing by rushing it. She was too special. No, he would wait until the time was right, no matter how many times he had to jerk himself off between then and now.

***

A few days later, Amber was deep into her regression. Malcolm praised her often, saying he was extremely happy with the progress that she had made, and it was true. She had taken to it like a natural, and it did his heart good to watch her become more playful and innocent with every passing day. She was using her diaper without hesitation, now, and depended on him for nearly everything. She looked to him to feed her, bathe her, and entertain her. Just as he had suspected from the beginning, she was the perfect submissive, and her every thought now revolved around pleasing him. It wasn't long before he decided that she was ready. She was his now, truly and completely. It was time to take their arrangement to the next level. He began by letting her dress in "big girl" clothes and letting her decide whether or not she felt like being diapered at any given time. He made it clear that it was her decision, but if she decided that she was in big girl mode within the apartment, she was to only wear skirts with no panties and no bra. Outside of the apartment, she could wear whatever she liked. That adjustment took a few days in and on itself as she experienced some mild anxiety around choosing how big or little she felt like being each day. He guided her through that phase with warmth and patience, assuring her that it was natural.

"You just need to get used to listening to your inner voice," he advised. "Most people never learn how to do that, not really, but it's a very important thing to master if you are going to be in a power exchange relationship." She bit her lip and nodded along, trying not to get too excited at the use of the word "relationship," telling herself that surely he meant it in a more general sense. They had never talked about it explicitly, but she was under the assumption that that sort of thing was off the table. The longer they spent together, the stronger her feelings for him grew into something stronger than boss/employee dynamic, even for such an unusual one as this. She kept these feelings to herself, however, not wanting to rock the boat lest he cancel the whole arrangement on the spot. She would rather have part of him than none of him, she decided.

Once she felt more comfortable with that phase, he began giving her more responsibilities, showing her the sort of tasks she would be completing as his personal assistant. At first, he only had her performing the tasks which would keep her inside, not wanting to overwhelm her with having to navigate the neighborhood and deal with strangers on top of all the other changes he was throwing at her. One thing at a time, he had insisted, and she was glad for it. Those things did sound awfully intimidating in her current state of mind.

"We'll start with my laundry," he said. "You will be responsible for washing, drying, ironing, and putting away my clothes." He explained the washer and dryer to her as she listened and nodded along as though she hadn't been doing laundry for her entire life. Something about the way that he explained everything to her as though she were just learning about it for the first time made her feel strangely turned on, and she suspected that he was doing it for similar reasons. He also made sure that she understood which fabrics could be machine washed, which had to be dry cleaned as well as which temperature and wash setting was appropriate for every item of clothing. Once he felt she was fully briefed, he gathered up the items he wanted her to attend to first.

"One more thing," he said with a twinkle in his eye. "You'll be wearing this." In his hand was a ball gag, which he held out to her. "Open," he said and placed it in her mouth, fastening it in place. She closed her lips around it, trying to find a comfortable way to hold it in her mouth. He stood back and admired the way she looked in the purple tank top and black skirt she had picked out for herself that morning, the black gag stood out in stark contrast to the cute outfit.

"There,' he said with a smile. "Now, you're perfect." He watched her as she moved around the laundry room, starting a new load of washing before tackling the pile of ironing. Something about the way that his eyes tracked her every movement told her that he loved to see her this way, attending to his needs. As she tried to accommodate the ball gag in her mouth, she found it hard to swallow. Try as she might try to contain it, drool was soon dripping down her chin and onto her pretty top. At first, she was embarrassed, thinking that surely he would think she was gross for drooling all over herself, but instead, he seemed to be rather turned on by it.

"Mmm, you look so sexy. Daddy's slutty little baby." The demeaning words only made her horny and proud, especially when he said it in such a sultry way. She stopped trying to hold it back, letting her spit fall freely down the front of her shirt. It made her tank top stick to her nipples in a rather alluring way, and she suddenly felt sexy again. Malcolm casually pulled his hard cock out as she began to iron his shirts. She froze when she saw it, her eyes bulging out wildly at the size of it. It was by far the biggest cock she had ever seen in person, and she was at once intimidated and aroused by it. On the one hand, she wasn't sure she had what it took to service a member that large but on the other hand, she wanted nothing more than to try.

"I didn't tell you to stop, did I little one?" he asked, his voice taking on a stern tone. She snapped out of her reverie, dutifully turning her attention back to his work shirts. She sprayed more starch and brought the iron down on the garment, all the time painfully aware that he was watching her and pleasuring himself. She longed to be the one to give him pleasure or at the very least, to be allowed to watch, but she was afraid that if she took her eyes away from the task at hand, she would burn his shirt. He continued to stroke himself as he watched her iron all of his shirts until they were perfect and crisp. Once that last one had been hung up, she stood before him, awaiting her next instructions.

"Come here," he said, his voice thick and raspy with lust. She complied, allowing herself to peek at his throbbing cock as she crossed the short distance between them. "Kneel." She knelt before him, hoping that he would remove her ballgag and allow her to suck on his thick, yummy cock. Or at the very least, give him a handjob. Anything to be of use to him.

"Look at me," he said. As their eyes met, he began to stroke his cock faster, frantically working himself to a climax. "Do you want to suck Daddy's cock, baby?" She nodded and made a desperate noise of affirmation. She did her best to convey to him with her eyes how much she wanted to taste him, to feel his hot cum shooting down her throat. He stroked her cheek with his free hand, and hope leaped up in her chest. To her dismay, however, he shook his head.

"You haven't earned that privilege yet, I'm afraid. Be a good girl and let Daddy cum on your face, and I'll consider letting you suck me off next time." She nodded eagerly, thrilled to be allowed to serve him in any way she could. He gripped her face harder as he neared his climax. It felt so strangely possessive, and her body thrilled at the contact. He slid his hand down and scooped up some of the drool that was hanging from her chin and used it to make his cock slick enough to stroke it faster. With a loud grunt, he sprayed his cum all over her face and tank top, soaking it further. Strangely, kneeling on the floor covered in spit and cum was the sexiest she had ever felt in her life. If someone had told her just a few weeks ago that she would be begging for some guy to cum all over her face, to be truly desperate for it, she would have laughed in their face. In just a short time she had transformed from a shy, inexperienced girl to a wanton, shameless slut. Even the thought of being a slut made her pussy ached. She longed for Malcolm to fuck her at last, but, as he said, she still had not earned that privilege. She vowed to do whatever it took to earn his cock. She would do anything if it meant relieving this terrible ache she had for him.

"Oh sweetheart, you look so sexy right now," he said, zipping his cock back into his pants. Indeed, she did feel sexy. His cum on her face seemed to mark her as his, and she wore it with pride. "Go clean yourself up, pumpkin. You can play in your room while Daddy gets dinner ready. No TV." She got up and skipped up to her room. Once she closed the door, she decided not to remove the ball gag or clean the cum off of her face right away. With a glance at the closed door, she slipped her hand under her skirt to find that her pussy was soaking wet. She touched her fingers to her face and scooped up a bit of his jizz and rubbed it over her clit. The sensation made her whole body shiver with fierce pleasure. She plunged her finger into her hungry pussy, fucking herself hard and fast. In her mind, she replayed what had just happened, how she had happily given her body up as a cum rag. She recalled him calling her a dumb baby, and the memory made her cum instantly. As waves of release washed over her, she moaned softly against the ball gag. Downstairs, Malcolm listened on the baby monitor as his baby girl made herself cum. She thought she was being quiet, but he heard every grunt and moan. He grinned at the knowledge that being used by him in such a degrading manner had made her so horny that she had to rush off and make herself cum immediately. From the sound of it, she hadn't even cleaned herself off first. He was so proud of her that he didn't even mind that she was touching herself without his permission. He idly rubbed his chin and decided that she was ready at last. He had her exactly where he wanted her.

Chapter 8

"Get ready, baby girl. We're going on a date," he announced the next afternoon. She had just woken up from her nap, and she was feeling a bit groggy, but the prospect of a date perked her right up.

"Really?!" She was so excited that she was practically squealing. It had been a couple of weeks since she had left the apartment. Maybe longer, it was hard to keep track when your days were filled with diaper changes and laundry duty. The prospect of getting to dress up and have some stimulating conversation thrilled her to the core.

"Yes, my dear. We'll be going to dinner and then to a movie. Would you like that?" Her response was to jump up and down, clapping her hands with joy. He laughed and looked at her with warm affection. Her innocence remained his favorite part about her.

"Good. Now go get ready, little one." He leaned in and whispered in her ear, his hot breath sending goosebumps all down her arms. "And make sure you shave every inch of your lovely body." Her pussy instantly flooded with desire, and she grinned at the implication. Would tonight be the night? Would the long wait finally be over?

"Yes, Daddy," she whispered in response. She scurried upstairs, her mind racing as she thought about which outfit she would wear and how she would do her hair and makeup. It had been such a long time since she had been on a date and this one was especially important to her, and she wanted to look especially nice.

If he wants to take me out, get to know me better, perhaps there is something more going on here, she dared to hope. He had a hold on her, unlike any man she had ever met before. All other men that she had dated before now seemed like boys in comparison to Malcolm. Although the logical, sensible part of her brain warned her that it was not a good idea, Amber knew that she was falling for him. She didn't know what a girl like her could offer a man like him except for her complete devotion. Everything would have to be perfect tonight. She took extra special care as she was getting ready. Not only did she shave herself completely bare, but she also did a full-body sugar scrub to get her skin as silky smooth as possible. She followed that up with a creamy lotion, getting herself so soft to the touch that even she couldn't stop running her hands over herself. Next, she styled her hair, carefully curling it and spraying it to perfection. She let it drape over shoulders, wanting to show off a more elegant side of herself this evening. She spent longer than usual on her makeup as well, even looking up a few tutorials online to make sure that she looked absolutely perfect for Malcolm. She had a feeling that he was used to a certain level of elegance in his women. For her clothes, she chose a simple low-cut black dress that hugged her curves perfectly. After some consideration, she decided that the only thing she would wear underneath was a pair of black silk thigh highs. As she studied herself in the mirror, she had to admit that she looked stunning. Her nipples stood at attention already, advertising the fact that she was braless, and she loved the feeling of the satiny material against her bare skin, thrilled with the knowledge that she was accessible to Malcolm at any moment should he choose to take her this evening. She hoped with all her heart that he would. All of this waiting was exquisite torture, but she longed to belong to him truly and completely. The last step was a pair of high heeled shoes. Amber stepped into them, grateful that she had taken the time to practice walking in them prior to wearing them out in public. They were a bit higher than she was used to but they looked so perfect with the rest of her outfit that she was happy to tolerate the slight discomfort. She was sure to grow used to them as the evening wore on.

At last, her outfit was complete, and she was ready. She practically floated down the stairs. Her excitement made her feel as light as a feather. Malcolm was waiting for her on the loveseat by the stairs, patiently flipping through a magazine. When he looked up at her, his face lit up so much that her heart did a little somersault in her chest. He looked incredible, as well, wearing a black suit so perfectly tailored that it hugged his toned figure as though it were made for him.

"Oh, little one," he breathed. "You look so beautiful. Come here let me look at you." She sauntered over to him, delighting in the way his eyes followed her every movement. As she twirled around slowly to let him see her from every angle, his eyes began to take on a hungry quality. He wrapped his hands around her waist, pulling her close to him. She felt her breath catch as she melted into his arms. He ran his hands over the silky fabric and pressed his forehead to hers. His hands traveled up her ribcage and brushed over her breasts, then up her neck and into her hair. At last, he pulled her in for a kiss, soft and deep. It was tentative at first, almost shy, but then his tongue was pushing into her mouth, demanding to taste her. She wrapped her arms around his neck, clinging to him as he explored her mouth. Their tongues danced together, and she found herself almost swooning with pleasure as he kissed her with a building passion. Suddenly, he broke off the kiss, leaving her stunned and breathless. He grinned down at her, and she found herself thinking that when she agreed to be tortured by him, this wasn't exactly what she had in mind.

"Hungry?" he asked cheerily and held his arm out for her to take. She was too dazed even to pout so she took his arm and let him lead her to the elevator. As they descended, he let his hand rest on the curve of her ass, and the casual possessiveness made her feel weak in the knees. A town car was waiting for them outside, and Malcolm held the door open for her to get in first. She slid into the back seat, excited at the chance to see how the other half lived. She had lived in the city for a couple of years now but had never really gotten the time or the money needed to really see the sights. Even dinner and a movie sounded thrilling to her after spending the last couple of years so focused on finding her big break. Not to mention, having a driver seemed like the height of luxury to her after splitting cabs or walking everywhere. As he slid in next to her, he wrapped his arm around her shoulders. She leaned her head against him, savoring his warmth and strength. She felt safer with him than she had with any other person save her parents. Deep down, she trusted him completely and knew that he would never let anything bad happen to her as long as he was around. They didn't talk much on the way to the restaurant but rather communicated silently with caresses and sighs. He ran his fingers over her knee and up her thigh, teasing her but never going as high up as she would have wanted. By the time they reached their destination, she was squirming in her seat, and her wetness was coating the inside of her legs. All she wanted was for him to fuck her right then and there in the car, but she knew that he was enjoying making her wait.

The restaurant was very upscale, and Amber felt a bit out of place. Luckily, Malcolm took the lead, indicating to her where to sit and helping her to navigate the French menu. He requested a secluded table in the corner where once seated, they were completely out of view of the rest of the restaurant thanks to some large potted plants and a strategically placed column, and it almost felt as though they were alone. When the waiter came by, Malcolm ordered drinks and hors d'oeuvres, and she let herself relax and enjoy the ambiance. It felt nice to relax and let someone else take care of the details. Malcolm ordered a bottle of champagne for the two of them to split.

"Now, show Daddy your pretty pink pussy," he said as soon as the waiter was out of earshot. Amber blushed and looked around nervously, but her knees were already parting. Her body responded to his command as though it were the most natural thing in the world. She lifted up the hem of her dress, exposing her freshly shaved pussy as he took her in with hungry eyes.

"Good girl," he smirked. "Now, touch yourself." This time, she hesitated. Surely the waiter would be back with their champagne at any moment. Sensing her reluctance, he leaned forward and gave her a stern look.

"Don't you want to be a good girl for Daddy?" She gulped and nodded, needing his approval more than anything. "Then do as I say and touch yourself." She took in a deep breath, steeled her resolve, and slid a finger up her smooth slit, already dewey with lust. It felt so nice as she twirled her finger around her tender button, Malcolm's eyes glued to her glistening folds, that she completely forgot that they were in public. That is until the waiter returned with their champagne. Amber let out an involuntary "eep" and pulled the hem of her dress down. She turned a deeper shade of red and did her best to avoid the gaze of the waiter, who quickly put their drinks down and left.

"Did I tell you you could stop?" he asked, his

voice carrying the unspoken threat of hard spankings.

"No, Daddy." She lifted her dress once more, fingers resuming their exploration of her private parts.

"Why do you look so embarrassed, little one? You're Daddy's little slave, and you don't care who knows it. Say it." She met his gaze shyly and did as he commanded.

"I'm Daddy's little slave, and I don't care who knows it." As the words came out of her mouth, she could feel her pussy get wetter. Being under his control was so intoxicating.

"Let Daddy taste how dripping wet you are." She reached out her fingers, slick with her juices, and he captured them in his mouth. As he tasted her, his lips curled into a seductive smile, and he made a satisfied "mmm." The sound made a subtle vibration on her fingertips, making her giggle a little.

"Good girl," he said, returning her hand to her lap. "Now drink your champagne." They toasted to a successful partnership, and the bubbles tickled Amber's nose as she drank.

"So," he said, putting his glass down again. "Tell me more about yourself, Amber. Tell me about your history." She almost giggled at the word "history" and the implication it carried that she had some grand story to tell. She told him about growing up in a quiet, small-town, always doing well in school, never one to get in trouble or rebel in any way. Then she told him about how she left home a few years back to pursue her dream of acting. He seemed surprised when she mentioned that last part.

"You've never mentioned that before," he said, leaning forward, his gaze suddenly shifting from curious to penetrating.

"Why not?"

"Well, it's on hold right now, obviously. I couldn't possibly have enough time to audition and do my job properly." He shook his head, hissing under his breath.

"No, that won't do at all," he said. "From

now on, auditioning for parts is now officially part of your work duties." For a moment, she was so stunned that she didn't know what to say.

"Really? Why would you want that?" It didn't really make sense to her why he would want her to do something that would interfere with her being available to him twenty-four-seven, something that he had made clear was very important to him.

"Because one of the main duties of a Daddy is making sure that his little is happy. It's my job to make sure that all of your needs are met, including your creative needs and your life goals. If acting is important to you then it's important to me too. Tomorrow, I expect you to start looking for casting calls, and I want a daily report on your progress." She blushed, feeling like the luckiest girl in the world. If she thought it was hard not to fall for him before, it was going to be next to impossible if he kept this up. She reached across the table and squeezed his hand.

"Thank you, Daddy," was all that she could

manage to say, she was so overwhelmed with emotion. She could only hope that her eyes and the touch of her hand could convey her gratitude better than her words. Hopefully, he would let her show him her gratitude in a more tangible way later in the evening.

"Of course, princess. If you tell me who you are going to be auditioning with, I'll put in a good word for you. I know a few people in show business." That made her frown.

"I'd rather you didn't do that. I'd rather get the part on my own merits." He raised an eyebrow at that but didn't seem to be angry.

"Integrity move, baby girl. I have to say I'm impressed by that. Not many people would pass up a chance to get an inside track to success." She shrugged, somewhat embarrassed by the compliment.

"I don't know that it's an integrity move per se. I just feel like I will enjoy my success more if its a result of my own talent and hard work." He smiled at that and shook his head in a bemused fashion.

"I think that says more about your integrity than you realize. But if you don't want me to interfere, then I won't. I still expect daily progress reports, however. And I assume that helping you to memorize your lines is considered an appropriate form of support?" She giggled with delight.

"I would love that!" He actually looked happy at the thought of helping her, and the sight of it made her heart melt. She knew then that it didn't really matter what his intentions were, she was already falling in love with him, and there was nothing she could do about it. It was already too late. He ordered their entrees and spent the rest of the meal filling her in on his past. He, too, was from a small town which she found surprising given his polished, cosmopolitan air. He had gotten into school on a scholarship and decided to go to law school to become a public defender. After doing that for a few years, he said that he felt drained and underappreciated. It was around then that he was approached by a private law firm who was impressed by his record. Due to his burnout, he agreed to come on as a consultant provided he was allowed to work from home most of the time.

"I found that I needed to seclude myself from humanity from a while after dealing with the worst of the worst for so long. I'm feeling much better these days. If I'm honest, my only reason for still working from home is that I'm spoiled. I just got used to it, and now I don't want to go back." They shared a laugh and then began to contemplate dessert. Amber was considering a chocolate cake that sounded particularly divine but wasn't sure she wanted to indulge. Malcolm shamelessly encouraged her to go for it.

"Why would you deny yourself the pleasure when it is so very delicious?" he asked, winking suggestively. She immediately felt her core clench with desire and wondered how he could manage to make her heart race with just a wink.

"Well, when you put it like that," she giggled, blushing ever so slightly. He ordered a slice for them to share, and she was very glad that he did because it was every bit as delicious as it had sounded. Even as she grew uncomfortably full, she still felt like it was worth every bite. As they left, she noticed that he left the waiter an especially large tip and she hoped that it would help to make up for anything he may or may not have seen.

Chapter 9

Even the movie theater he took her too was upscale compared to what she was used to, stadium seating, and a huge IMAX screen. On the few occasions when she ventured out to the movies, it was always to the dollar theater. Malcolm insisted that they sit in the back and as the lights went down, she began to see why. He lifted the armrest that was between them and started caressing her knee, slowly making his way up her thigh. Her breath quickened, and her eyes darted around the sparsely populated theater. No one was sitting near them, and there was no reason why anyone should notice that he was getting handsy as long as she managed to keep quiet. She opened her legs wider, giving him access to her hungry pussy. As his fingers brushed against her folds, it was harder to suppress a cry of pleasure than she had imagined. His fingers explored her wetness, seeking out her already swollen clit. She bit her lip to hold back the wanton moan that wanted to escape as he teased her lightly.

"Does that feel good, princess?" he teased, murmuring quietly in her ear. She could only nod and grip the armrest on the other side of her to try to maintain her composure. As good as it felt, she longed to have his fingers inside of her, or better yet, his cock, the light pressure on her clit not nearly enough to ease her ache. If anything, it was making it worse.

"What's that?" he prompted. "I couldn't hear you over the movie." As he spoke, he continued to stimulate her, driving her wild with pleasure. It was taking all of her mental energy not to cry out in ecstasy and blow their cover. She burned with embarrassment as she imagined being thrown out of the theater for lewd acts. When she didn't answer right away, he fisted his hand into her hair, pulling it hard enough to force her head back. He leaned in and whispered in her ear, his tone growing impatient.

"I asked you a question, little girl. If you don't answer me, you will regret it when we get back home." She clenched her eyes closed, shutting out everything else in an effort to concentrate.

"Yes, Daddy," she managed to whisper. "That feels so good."

"Good," he growled and tightened his grip on her hair. She gasped, but the music playing under the action scene drowned it out. "Is this what you've been craving, little one?"

"Yes, Daddy," she whimpered. His finger began to travel down, teasing her entrance. She shivered in anticipation, but he didn't give her what she craved, not yet. She was beginning to wonder if she would ever get satisfaction.

"You're so wet, pumpkin. I bet that's not all you've been craving. Why don't you tell Daddy all about it?" She took a deep breath and opened her eyes, peeking to see if anyone had noticed their naughty little game. Everyone seemed fixated on the movie, and so she focused her concentration on answering him.

"I've been craving your cock," she whispered, grateful that no one could see her blush.

"What else?" he hissed in her ear.

"Fucking you. I want to fuck you so bad, Daddy." By now, she was such a horny, dripping mess that she didn't care who saw or heard. All that mattered was the finger between her legs and the heaven it promised.

"I know you have. Look at you. You're just a squirming, whimpering little slut so desperate for her Daddy's cock that she'll let him finger her in public. Isn't that right?" His teasing words only made her situation worse, made her pussy ache for him.

"Yes, Daddy. Please finger my desperate little cunt." With a growl of approval, he plunged his finger in at last, and she took it all, struggling not to scream out with satisfaction. As he finger fucked her, it felt so amazing that she had to clamp her hand down over her mouth to muffle the soft noises of pleasure that she couldn't hold back. With every thrust, she saw stars behind her closed eyes and felt herself building quickly to a climax.

"You're not about to cum already, are you pumpkin? Right here in front of all of these people? Are you really that much of greedy little slut? How cute." She couldn't hold it back anymore. She gripped the armrest as powerful waves of ecstasy washed over her. Somehow, she managed not to make a sound louder than a whimper as she came. When her body relaxed once again, Malcolm finally let go of the grip he had on her hair and pulled her to him for a kiss. Her breath was still shaky, but it soon stilled again as their tongues met over and over. The kiss grew deeper as though he couldn't get enough of her. His hands began to wander over her thighs, up her hips and waist, seeking out her breasts. He tweaked her nipples beneath the thin material of the dress, making them stand at attention. Already, she could feel the heat building between her legs again, her desire for him far from sated. As their making outreached a frenzied state, the credits began to roll on the movie. Amber dimly thought that she didn't see a single second of the film and had no idea what it was even about. Malcolm took her by the hand and began to lead her toward the exit.

"Come one, kitten. Let's get you home and in Daddy's bed."

Chapter 10

He couldn't keep his hands off of her in the car, raising the partition between them and the driver so that he could freely explore her body, kissing her neck and breasts. She moaned and gripped his broad shoulders, wishing that the driver would go faster so that they could be back in their little love nest. He couldn't stop kissing her in the elevator either, devouring her with all of the passion that had built up between them over the past few weeks. As soon as the elevator doors opened, he picked her up and carried her over the threshold, up the stairs, and directly to his bedroom. She had never been in his room before but didn't really get a chance to admire it as they tumbled onto the bed together, already pulling off one another's clothes. He tugged at her dress so impatiently that it ripped.

"I'll buy you another one," he growled as if she could give a shit about the dress. Luckily, she didn't have anything on underneath for him to ruin in his haste. She was more careful with his jacket and shirt and only got his shirt halfway unbuttoned before he ripped that off as well, sending buttons flying. She had a sneaking suspicion that she would be tasked with sewing those back on once they had cooled down. He settled his weight down on top of her, spreading her legs with his knee. For a moment, he only studied her closely as though trying to memorize her face, stroking her cheek with his thumb. She was mesmerized by his gaze, even as her body burned for more.

"You're mine, completely mine. Say it."

"I'm completely yours." As she said it, she realized how deeply she meant it. She had given her heart and mind to him, and now it was time to give her body as well. He sighed and kissed her with a tenderness that surprised her. Slowly, the kiss deepened once more, and she could feel his erection pressing into her. She fumbled with his belt but didn't make any progress. Finally, he took over, removing his pants and underwear, kicking them off to the side. At the sight of his large member, a small shiver of anticipation went through her. The moment that she had been dreaming of was finally here. He was hers. She reverently ran her hands over his well-muscled figure. His body was like a work of art, and she was so grateful to at last have the chance to touch him. He, too, ran his hands over her body, seeming to know instinctively all of her pleasure points. He began to rub his hard cock over her slick folds, making her cry out with pleasure and an aching desire for more.

"Oh, baby girl. You're so beautiful." As he ran the tip of his cock over her clit, she dug her nails into his back. Her earlier orgasm only made her more sensitive, and having his cock, so close was driving her wild. He kissed her neck tenderly, not seeming to notice her impatience to have him inside of her. He seemed to prefer to take his time and savor her instead. She ran her hands down his brawny back and to his firm buttocks, pulling him closer to her. She had savored him more than enough, she felt, now she needed to get fucked.

"You want Daddy's cock that bad, little one?" he teased and then nibbled her earlobe, sending a jolt of electric pleasure throughout her body. She moaned loudly and moved her hips, seeking to find the angle which would allow him access.

"I want your cock so bad," she moaned, too horny to care if she sounded desperate. She was desperate, desperate to have him at last. "Please fuck me, Daddy. I need you." His only response was a happy sigh before he plunged himself inside of her at last. She cried out with relief and delight as his thick cock stretched her open, filling her up more completely than anyone ever had before. His girth was so large that it was slightly uncomfortable, but she found that the mild pain only heightened her pleasure. She opened her legs wider, wanting to take him deeper inside of her, wanting to feel every inch of him. It felt so good to be claimed by him at last, and every thrust felt like an affirmation that she belonged to him.

"Fuck, you feel so good," he growled, driving into her harder. "You're so perfect." She was too lost in her own pleasure to respond with anything other than a loud moan. She bucked her hips upward to meet his, every thrust bringing her closer to another orgasm. Never before had anyone fucked her so passionately, and it was driving her to heights of pleasure that she didn't even know existed.

"You're so tight, little one. Are you going to cum for Daddy again?" His voice with thick with lust and something else, amusement perhaps. He slowed to an agonizingly slow pace, and she could feel her needy pussy pulsing around him, crying out for the climax that had been rapidly approaching. He grinned down at her, clearly enjoying torturing her. She groaned and gripped his buttocks, trying to coax him back into the fast and hard rhythm that she craved so badly.

"Please, Daddy. Please …" she cried but to no avail. His slow movements felt wonderful but were not what she needed. What she needed was that hard pounding rhythm, the dominant insistence that she submit to the pleasure he desired her to have.

"Poor greedy little slut," he teased, prolonging her torture. "You're already begging for Daddy to let you cum, aren't you?"

"Y-yes, please! Please let me cum, Daddy." He was done teasing her. He pounded into her with such force that she immediately came undone beneath him. Her fingers clawed at the air, and she felt for a moment that she might lose her mind. Her body shook with waves of pleasure so intense that she couldn't even form a sound. She could only grip him with her thighs until the waves stopped.

"Oh princess," he whispered as she collapsed against the mattress, her limbs feeling like they had turned to jelly. He once again slowed down his pace and captured her lips with his with a shaky sigh. She melted open for him, feeling more sated and more complete than she ever had before. He cupped her face with his hands, slowly but steadily pumping into her as they kissed. "You're such a good girl. My perfect girl." Suddenly, he pulled out of her, deftly flipping her over onto her stomach. He pulled her hips up and plunged into her once again. The change of position seemed to make her body come alive with the new sensations. His thick cock stretched her open and seemed to hit all the right spots every time he hammered into her. She gripped the pillows, holding on as he rutted into her like a frenzied animal. He no longer seemed to care about savoring it. He grabbed a fistful of her hair, and she felt so owned by him, so used in a deliciously sexy way. No longer did he seem to care about her pleasure. She was there to service him, to service his cock and it filled her with a deep sense of pride. At last, she could feel his cock swelling inside of her, and she knew that she was about to receive her reward finally. With a loud groan, he unloaded himself, pumping her full of his hot seed, the sensation making her toes curl. He collapsed his weight against her, and together, they fell onto the mattress in a sweaty, panting heap. They lay like that for several minutes, both of them completely satisfied and too spent to move. Eventually, he rolled off of her and pulled her to him, wrapping her tightly in his arms. They kissed, no less passionately now that they had had their fill of one another than they had before. If anything, she felt as though experiencing how good it could be between them only served to heighten her craving for him. When he broke off the kiss, she whimpered with disappointment. He chuckled and kissed her lightly on the forehead.

"Go to sleep, little one," he whispered into her hair. "There will be plenty of time for all of that in the morning. Get your rest, my dear." She quieted, knowing that he was right. Her body was sore and exhausted, and recharging seemed like the sensible thing to do. She willed her body to settle down, and she relaxed into his warmth. As he pulled the covers over them, she was already yawning.

"Good night, Daddy," she murmured and wrapped her arms around him as tightly as she could as though he were one of her stuffies.

"Good night, princess."

Chapter 11

When she awoke the next morning, Malcolm was already up. She heard him banging around in the kitchen and whistling a happy tune all the way from upstairs. It was a sound that filled her heart with joy. She stretched out on the luxurious linens and took a moment to bask in her own happiness. The previous night felt like a wonderful dream, except the wetness between her legs and Malcolm's cheery tune assured it that it was very real. After a bit of a lie-in, she reluctantly got out of his bed and padded to her room, still naked. She picked out her outfit for the day, opting for a very short mini skirt and a crop top, adhering to the no bra or panty rule. She washed the makeup from last off of her face and brushed her hair, then went downstairs to greet Malcolm.

"Good morning, princess." He greeted her

with a grin and a kiss on the forehead. "You are looking especially sexy this morning." He grabbed her bare ass under her skirt, squeezing it hard as he pulled her against him.

"Thank you, Daddy," she answered, her voice a little breathless from the butterflies she felt as he handled her so possessively.

"Breakfast is ready," he said with a wink. "You had better eat up. We have a very busy day ahead of us." She sat at the table on most days now, only eating in her high chair when she was feeling particularly like being coddled. He served up scrambled eggs and toast with coffee. As soon as the first bite hit her lips, she realized how ravenous she was. She was so hungry that she even had seconds. As she put her fork down, at last, she noticed that he was looking at her with an odd twinkle in his eyes.

"All done?" She nodded with a satisfied smile on her face. "Good. You're on dish duty this morning." Something about the way he looked at her when he said it made her look forward to it.

She wondered what devious plan he had cooked up.

"Yes, Daddy," she said, making her voice low and seductive. She gathered up their dirty dishes and took them to the sink. As she rinsed them off, she felt his hands encircle her waist. He pressed his already hard member against her ass, making her gasp as a desperate need to have him gripped her body.

"Don't stop, little one," he whispered in her ear. With a great deal of effort, she returned her focus to the task at hand. His hands slid under her skirt and once again squeezed her bare ass, his fingers digging into her soft flesh. She let out a soft moan and could feel herself getting wet. As he spread her cheeks open, she found it difficult to keep her concentration on the plate she was washing. That earned her a slap on the ass, making her yelp in surprise. It was a lot more painful when there was no diaper there to dampen the blow.

"I said not to stop, didn't I?" he growled.

"Sorry, Daddy," she whimpered, the mild

burning of her ass cheek only serving to make her more horny for him. He slipped his finger between her moist folds, making a noise of satisfaction at the wetness he found there. This time, she remembered to continue to wash the plate despite the jolt of pleasure coming from between her legs.

"You don't seem very sorry. You seem like a desperate little slut to me. Aren't you baby girl?" She slowly ran a sponge across the plate, using all of her concentration to focus on what she had been told to do. It wasn't enough, however, and he smacked her ass again, harder, making her hiss at the pain.

"I asked you a question, baby girl," he growled and spanked her ass one more time to drive home his point. She chided herself, not focussing harder, wishing she could be better for him.

"Yes, Daddy. I am a desperate little slut." At last, the plate was clean. She rinsed it off and put it to the side. With shaky fingers, she picked up the next one and began to clean it as well.

"Good girl," he said. "I'm glad that you know what you are. My domesticated little fuck slave." The words made her shiver with delight. She heard the sound of metal on metal and knew that he was unzipping his pants, and she longed to have him inside of her. He nestled his hard cock between her cheeks and growled into her ear.

"Say it."

"I'm your domesticated little fuck slave." Her words almost came as moans. She whimpered as he began to slide his hard cock closer to her entrance, teasing her. It was so difficult to keep her attention on washing the dishes, but she was doing her best. She finished the plate that she was working on and moved on to the pots and pans.

"That's right," he said. "You are here to serve me." With that, he pushed himself inside of her, burying himself deep within her with one thrust. She gasped as his huge cock stretched her open and nearly dropped the pot that she was cleaning. He didn't seem to notice. He was too busy pounding into her.

"Oh, sweetie," he said. "Your pussy is so tight. I love fucking you." He was fucking her so hard and so fast, clearly intent on using her body to pleasure himself. She found his control over her to be so deliciously erotic, and every thrust sent a lightning bolt of pleasure through her.

"You're Daddy's good little slut," he snarled. Suddenly, he was pulsing inside of her, grunting loudly as he came. His hot cum felt so wonderful inside of her that her eyes rolled back. He slowly pumped into her a few more times before pulling out. As his semen dripped out of her, she almost felt a sense of regret, wanting to keep him inside of her for longer. He zipped himself up, but he wasn't done with her yet.

"Finish up these dishes and report to my office when you're done," he said, giving her ass one final smack before walking away.

Chapter 12

She finished the few remaining dishes as quickly as she could. Nervously, she smoothed her hair and skirt, wondering what he had in store for her next. She left the semen that was dripping down her leg, loving how dirty it made her feel. She had a feeling that Malcolm would feel the same way. He was working at his desk when she came into his office, a coil of rope sitting on the desk next to his computer. He gestured toward the velvet settee opposite his desk, indicating that she should sit. She sat and waited several moments before he reached a stopping point with his work. She had grown accustomed to being made to wait by now. Finally, he picked up the rope and came over to where she was sitting. Without a word of explanation, he began to tie her hands behind her back. Then, he wrapped the rope around her thighs, arranging her so that her legs were forced up and open, leaving her pussy exposed for his viewing pleasure. He stepped back to his desk to retrieve two items, a small vibrator, and a ball gag. He slid the vibrator into her pussy, making her shiver and make a small noise of pleasure. She was still slick with his cum, and it slid in quite easily. It was an unusual design, curving back onto itself so that it stimulated both the g-spot and the clitoris at the same time. Lastly, he slid the ball gag over her head, fastening it into place. She was completely helpless, completely at his mercy. He could do whatever he wanted to her, and the thought made her pussy ache.

"Well, don't you look absolutely perfect. Daddy's perfect little fucktoy. Now, let's try this out." He took out his phone and tapped the screen a few times. She felt a powerful vibration between her legs, making her legs quiver. A little squeak escaped her lips from behind the ball gag as it hit both of her most sensitive areas at once. He watched her intently, letting the vibrator go on for several seconds before stopping it with a few more taps on his phone.

"You are mine, and I will play with you whenever and wherever I wish. I control that greedy little pussy of yours now. Is that understood?" She nodded and made a noise of affirmation, her breath quickening at the thought of being controlled by him so literally. With this little gadget, he could give or deny her pleasure at the touch of a button.

"Good girl. Now sit there and look pretty for Daddy," he said and went back to sit at his desk. She waited for what felt like an eternity, her entire body tingling in anticipation. He had aroused her desire when he fucked her earlier and sitting here with her pussy exposed, bound in place. It was only growing stronger. She began to squirm, desperate for stimulation, but still, he ignored her and continued on with his work.

At last, he stopped and turned to her again. He made no moves towards her, only stared at her for a long while, as though she were a piece of art in a museum to be studied. At last, he smirked and picked up his phone.

"I see you squirming over there, little one," he teased. "Greedy for more?" She felt the vibe come to life between her legs and made a choked cry, muffled by the ball gag. He turned the vibe off again, looking very pleased with himself. "That's the lowest setting, by the way. There are many more powerful settings than that." She shivered in anticipation, waiting for him to turn the vibe on once more. He kept her waiting, however, turning his attention back to his work. She wondered vaguely if he was even working on anything or if it was an elaborate ruse designed to drive her mad. If it was, it was working. She decided as she began to squirm again. The thought was cut short as the vibe came back, even stronger than before. She hadn't even seen him move that time, and it caught her completely off guard. Her muscles tensed as the strong sensation had her immediately on the verge of an orgasm. She was all too aware that he hadn't given her permission to cum, however, and she held herself back somehow. Just as she thought she couldn't hold back any longer, he suddenly turned the vibe off again. She sat there panting, her pussy clenching around the vibe, seeking the orgasm it had been denied.

"You look so cute like that," he sneered. "Legs wide open like the greedy slut you are, unable to hide how desperately horny you are. I know you want to cum, don't you, princess?" She nodded, pleading with him with her eyes. She wanted to cum more than anything in the world. The vibe came back to life, and Amber couldn't even think as her orgasm came roaring back. Her body tensed up, trying desperately to keep from cumming without permission. As he turned it off again, she relaxed against the settee, panting and sweaty.

"You didn't cum, did you little one?" he growled, and she shook head. Despite how desperately she wanted to, she was still his obedient little fuck-slave, and she would hold off as long as she could.

"Good girl," he purred. "That's Daddy pussy, his toy. Isn't that right?" She couldn't even nod as he turned the vibe up yet another level. She made wild, keening noises, wordlessly begging him to allow her to release. He turned it off again and unzipped his pants, taking out his hard cock. He stroked himself as he watched her, breathlessly squirming on the settee. He watched her for so long. She wondered if he was going to jerk himself off, leaving her unsatisfied yet again. She couldn't even see his cock from where he sat, denied even the satisfaction of watching him pleasure himself. Finally, he stood, cock in hand, and came over to where she sat. He removed the ball gag and slid his cock past her lips, groaning with satisfaction as she swallowed his swollen member. He tapped his phone, bringing the vibe on again.

"I know you want to cum, baby girl. Luckily for you, I'm very pleased with your behavior so far today. You can cum as many times as you want as you deepthroat Daddy. Go on, let it out." He turned up the intensity as he spoke, simultaneously pushing himself further and further down her throat. She couldn't hold it in anymore. As her climax shook her body, her eyes rolled back in her head. He kept right on fucking her throat, growling with satisfaction as her body convulsed with ecstasy. She was so lost in her orgasm that his thick cock slid effortlessly down her throat.

"There, isn't that better, kitten?" he taunted, pulling his cock out long enough for her to catch her breath. She couldn't respond, however, as the vibe was still going strong, sending aftershocks rippling all through her body. Her first orgasm had barely finished when a second one came crashing over her, and he pushed himself back down her throat as she came, wanting her to associate having his cock down her throat with the powerful orgasm that ripped through her body. He gripped the back of her head, pulling her further onto his shaft as she choked and whimpered around him. She fought to take his girth down her throat, loving the way it made her feel, how it only added to the heavenly sensations between her legs. Just when she thought she might lose her mind from the pleasure, he turned the vibe back off. He didn't stop fucking her throat, however, grunting as her eyes rolled back in her head, and she felt her mind go completely blank. She was just a vessel for his pleasure now, capable only of doing what she was told. He looked down at her with a smirk, knowing that she was deep in subspace by now. He turned the vibe back on as high as it would go, curious how many times he could make her cum. As her eyes fluttered closed, he changed the setting again, making the vibe pulse on and off in an undulating pattern. She found the change of stimulation to be even more arousing and she enthusiastically bobbed her head up and down on his cock, surrendering to him completely. He turned the vibe up to the third level, this time at a strong and steady pulse. She could feel yet another orgasm building and knew it wouldn't be long before it came crashing over her. Just for fun, he cut the vibe off just as she was on the edge of cumming. She whimpered with disappointment and squirmed, trying desperately to stimulate her aching pussy.

"Poor, cum drunk little slut," he laughed, stroking her cheek adoringly. "You've already cum so many times, and you still want more."

"Yes, please," she murmured, her lips brushing against his cock as she spoke.

"Well, since you asked so nicely," he quipped and brought the vibe to life at its highest setting. Before she could even form a thought, she was already cumming again. As her orgasm receded, she expected him to turn the vibe off, but he did not. He only fucked her throat savagely, She could feel some drool begin to dribble out of her mouth and down his shaft, but she was so drunk on lust that she didn't care. She was beyond all words and all thought. He was in control, and she was his puppet. As he thrust into her throat hard and fast, she climaxed again and again, losing track of how many times she came. It seemed to go on forever.

"Daddy's dirty little cocksucker," he

growled, his growing stiffer. "You're going to make me cum, princess." He grabbed her by her hair, pulling her off his shaft and looming over her. He worked his cock furiously over her open mouth and let loose all over her face. It was sensual and erotic, the way his hot seed rained down over her, and she caught as much as she could in her mouth, savoring the taste of him. He sighed with satisfaction as his orgasm receded. Still gripping her tightly by the hair, he brought her face to his, kissing her deeply as his ragged breath returned to a normal pace.

"Oh kitten, you look so pretty covered in my cum."

"Thank you, Daddy," she said, glowing at the compliment. Indeed, she did feel pretty, even tied up and coated with sticky cum. If that was how he liked her, then she was proud to oblige him. He scooped some of it off of her face, feeding it to her with his fingers, smirking at the way she eagerly gobbled it up. He left most of it on her face, her badge of honor, and put the ball gag back into her mouth and zipped himself up again.

"Stay just like that, princess," he said, as if she had any choice in the matter, and turned his attention back to his work.

Chapter 13

He kept her like that for a long time until her muscles ached, and she began to grow restless. Occasionally, he watched her squirm against her restraints, seemingly lost in thought but then he would return his attention to his work and ignore her once more. Finally, he turned his computer off and crossed the short distance from the desk to the settee. He took a moment to admire her one last time, bound and helpless, before gently removing the ball gag. She stretched her aching jaw, happy to be free.

"You did a very good job today, kitten," he said gently as he began to untie her. "Daddy is very proud of you." His praise made the sore muscles in her thighs more than worth it. Once she was freed from the rope, she stretched her limbs as well. With a quick kiss on her forehead, he bundled her up in his arms and carried her off to the bathroom. He drew a bubble bath for her, holding her hand as she got in, her legs still shaky. The warm water felt amazing on her stiff muscles, and she leaned back, surrendering to the relaxing sensations. His large hands began to massage her scalp, sending her even further into relaxed bliss. He moved his hands down to her shoulders, kneading the tense muscles until they released under his strong grip. Once she was in a total zenlike state, he cleaned her from head to toe with a loofah, carefully washing away all of the cum and sweat from her skin. He washed her hair next, rinsing out the suds with some water from a plastic cup. She leaned back, letting the warm water cascade over her hair. Once she was all clean, he spent some time rubbing her feet, letting her relax in the warm water while he eased any remaining tension away. Eventually, he let out the water and bundled her body and hair into towels before carrying her to her grownup bed.

As he lowered her onto the bed, he lowered

himself on top of her and kissed her lips, her petite frame melting against him, her soft tongue tenderly seeking out his. His hands cupped her cheeks, savoring her for a moment, before lowering them down to wrap around her throat. Instantly, her entire body was flooded with hot desire. Malcolm could feel the needful heat radiating off her skin as he tightened his grip. Her hands sought out his cock, caressing the length of his hardness through his pants as he choked her. He parted her legs by forcing his knees between them. In her relaxed state, Amber couldn't stop herself from rubbing her aching pussy against his thigh like an animal in heat. He chuckled and watched her writhe against him with satisfaction.

"Still greedy, my pet?" he growled into her ear. She nodded. He released her throat and brought his cock to her lips. "I want your mouth again. Suck my cock, my dirty girl." She obeyed, moaning at the taste of him. He put his hands on the back of her head, guiding the pace and the depth as she relaxed and let him fuck her throat.

She wanted to touch herself, but he knew she would wait until he gave her permission.

"Good slut," he said, letting her know just how proud he was of her. Her eyes rolled back in her head, his words making her pussy feel like it was on fire. He withdrew his cock from her mouth and placed it between her ample tits. Slick with her saliva, he began to slide it between them.

"You may touch yourself," he said, knowing that being used like this would drive her wild. He squeezed her tits tight around his member and let himself enjoy her body. "Good girl. Such a good girl." The sight of his hard cock disappearing into her cleavage over and over was just too sexy, and he felt himself getting close to the edge. Too close. He pulled his cock back and wrapped his hands around her throat once again.

"Fuck yourself," he commanded, and she plunged her fingers into her cunt, pumping them in and out furiously. She was quickly approaching the edge, as well.

"You want to cum, kitten?" he asked

teasingly. She nodded and fucked herself faster.

"Stop!" At his command, her hands left her cunt, and her entire being shuddered at the sudden interruption.

"That was a question, not an order. Do you want to cum?"

"Yes, Daddy,' she whimpered.

"Good girl. You may cum on my cock," he said. She turned around and got on all fours. He knelt and entered swiftly, impatient to be inside of her again. She had the tightest pussy he had ever fucked, not to mention the fact that her enthusiasm was very addictive. It was tempting to unload inside of her then and there, but he wanted to make her cum one last time before her nap. Pounding into her, he could feel pussy tighten as her orgasm began to surface, but he wanted to make it last just a little while longer, torment her with pleasure just a little bit longer. Finally, he couldn't hold back any longer.

"Cum now!" he commanded, and he could

feel her tighten and shudder against him in relief. He let go too, throwing his head back as they pulsed and quivered together. She was already yawning as he eased her onto the covers, wrapping them around her burrito style. He kissed her on the cheek and watched her for a moment, her face already slack with exhaustion. He had completely worn her out.

"Enjoy your nap, little one," he whispered. "You earned it."

***

She awoke sometime later to a dark and silent room. She listened for him but didn't hear anything outside of the room either. She didn't get up right away, spending some time to reflect on what happened earlier. It was almost like having someone else's memories as she remembered how wanton she had been, so completely uninhibited. She had never done anything that wild before. The memory made her grow hungry once again, despite how many times she had orgasmed that day. Daddy had called her so many dirty things as he used her, and she had loved every moment of it. The way that he degraded her and used her as a toy was so erotic. The memory made her moan, and her fingers dipped down to her pussy before she could catch herself. She was still slick with his cum, which only made her hornier. She told herself it was only for a second, but she couldn't bring herself to stop touching it. Warm waves of pleasure washed over her as she flicked the tender nub with her fingertip. Riding closer and closer to the edge, she closed her eyes and let herself enjoy the sensations.

I'll stop before I cum like a good girl. She promised herself silently. *Just another couple of seconds.*

"Stop!" Malcolm's voice was loud and angry. She jerked her hand away and opened her eyes to see him standing at the foot of her bed, frowning with his hands on his hips. He was shirtless and only wearing a pair of black pressed slacks, water still dripping from his hair as though he had just stepped out of the shower.

"Bad girl!"

"Daddy! I- I-" she stuttered, knowing that she had been caught red-handed and wouldn't be able to talk her way out of it.

"Did I give you permission to touch yourself?" She did her best to ignore how sexy he looked with wet hair and no shirt and answered him in a quiet, shy voice.

"No, Daddy." She avoided his gaze, her face growing hot with shame.

"No, I certainly did not. Then why do you have your fingers in Daddy's toy? I'm sorry to have to do this, but you've been a very naughty little girl, and Daddy is going to have to punish you." He scooped her up in his arms, still naked, and carried her to her little girl room. There, he put her down firmly on one of the chairs surrounding the small table, and Amber chewed on her lip and wondered what kind of punishment he had in mind. He grabbed a notepad and a brown crayon from the shelf, both of which he put down on the table in front of her. Even his color choice was a punishment, she noticed.

"Write this down: 'I will not touch myself without Daddy's permission.'" Picking up the crayon with a shaky hand, she wrote the words down slowly and carefully. He watched over her shoulder and gave a single short nod when she had finished.

"Good. Now, I want you to write that forty times. Don't leave this chair until it's done. Bring it to me when you finish." He left her to begin her task and closed the door behind him. Obediently, Amber began copying the words. The crayon made the letters look sloppy and childish, which seemed fitting to her. She made sure to go slowly and take her time, not wanting to make any mistakes. Despite her best efforts, she did make a mistake on the sixteenth line, writing an "a" instead of an "o." She tore the page out and crumpled it up, starting again on a fresh sheet of paper. By the time she reached line thirty, her hand began to cramp.

Determined to push through the discomfort, she finished the second draft with no mistakes. Breathing a sigh of relief, she stood and got dressed, picking out an especially cute outfit in the hopes that it would earn her a little extra credit. She picked up the completed assignment, carrying it down the hall to present to Malcolm. He was sitting on the couch in the living room reading a newspaper, which he put down when Amber presented him with her work. He studied it carefully, reading it line by line. As he read, she noticed that he was now wearing a crisp button-down and that his hair had been neatly combed into place. Once he finished, he nodded and put it down.

"The second part of your punishment is to receive forty lashes with a belt on your bottom." Amber's jaw went slack with surprise.

"F-forty?!" she stuttered. Her tummy suddenly felt all fluttery, and her palms prickled with sweat.

"That's right. Bad girls who touch

themselves have to learn their lesson." He stood and removed his belt slowly, the leather making a wsssk sound as it passed through the loops on his trousers. As nervous as she was about her forty licks, the sight did excite her just a little. He sat back down again and motioned to his lap.

"Get over Daddy's knee, little girl." She swallowed nervously but did as she was told. As she settled onto his lap, he lifted up her skirt, exposing her bare bottom. He ran his hands over her flesh, raising goosebumps as he did so.

"Every time Daddy gives you a lick, I want you to count. Do you understand?"

"Yes, Daddy," she said. Without any further warning, he brought the belt down hard, exploding sharp pain onto her tender skin. Hot tears sprang to her eyes, and she gasped out loud.

"One," she managed to choke out, despite the sob trying to escape. The second blow came quickly, causing her to jerk from the burning pain.

"Two," she sobbed, squirming in his lap as he delivered blow after blow. She counted each one out loud, kicking and crying the entire time. The more she cried and squirmed and kicked, the harder she could feel Daddy's cock grow against her stomach. By the time he was through, her ass was bright red and covered in welts. He ran his hands lightly over her bruised skin, breathing heavily as he examined his handiwork. His fingers delved into her folds, groaning at the wetness he found there.

"Oh kitten, did your spanking make you horny?"

"Yes, Daddy," she confessed, hoping that wouldn't make him want to come up with a different way to punish her instead.

"Good," he said curtly. "Now, bend over." She bent over the couch, putting her hands down on the cushions but that wasn't what he had in mind. He pushed her face down into the couch cushions and got behind her. With her butt stuck up in the air, she felt incredibly exposed and vulnerable. She shivered with anticipation, wondering what he would do next. He hiked up her skirt and spread her stinging cheeks. She felt his hot, wet tongue against her pussy lips. He moaned as he explored her wet folds, enjoying the taste of her for a moment before working his way up. The tip of his tongue flicked against her bum, making her gasp. He spread her cheeks apart, burying his face deeper. His fingers digging into her bruised flesh stung but the pain only made the pleasure all the sweeter. A little moan escaped her lips as she leaned back onto that hot, wet tongue as it awoke a desire in her that she had never felt before. Once her rear entrance was nice and wet, he began to explore her with his fingers, stretching out her little hole bit by bit. She groaned and pushed back onto his exploring digits, craving more.

"You like that, naughty girl?" he asked.

"Yes, Daddy."

"Are you ready to take Daddy's cock in your ass?" He pulled his fingers out and started rubbing the head of his cock against her opening. She hesitated, wanting to feel that monster cock inside of her but also feeling a bit trepidatious.

"It's so big, Daddy. Will it fit?"

"Don't worry. I'll make it fit." The head of his cock slowly began to enter her and Amber tried her best to relax into it. Pain and pleasure swirled together in an intoxicating cocktail as she took deep breaths. He paused, barely inside of her and let her body adjust to this new intrusion.

"That's it, baby girl. Just relax and let Daddy in." He began to push a little further in, making her gasp as he stretched her tight asshole open. His fingers gripped her buttocks, spreading her flesh apart as he slowly impaled her. As he went deeper, she could feel herself relaxing more, accepting his presence in her virgin ass, and the pleasure started to become the dominant sensation over the pain.

"Oh princess, your ass is so tight around Daddy's cock!" he cried out, thrusting into her. He was finally entirely enveloped by her, and he started to very slowly pump in and out of her with small movements. Amber groaned loudly, feeling like he was going to split her in two. She had never felt so stretched, so filled. His strokes began to get a little longer, and Amber felt the need for release. Her moans must have betrayed her because he gave her a warning smack on the ass.

"No cumming, little one. You're still in trouble." Amber whimpered in disappointment. His cock felt so good, and she was so turned on, but she knew that she must be a good girl if she was going to get back into his good graces. "Now, take your ass fucking like a good little slut." He was fucking her hard and fast now, every stroke sending waves of pleasure all over her body. The way he grunted and cussed told Amber that he wouldn't last much longer. Sure enough, he gripped her by the hair and pulled her back onto his cock as he slammed into her. The combination of pain and ecstasy almost sent her over the edge, but she held back.

"Fuck, Daddy's going to cum in your tight little ass, princess!" She gasped as his cock swelled and twitched, pumping hot jizz deep inside of her. He shuddered and leaned all of his weight onto her, pinning her against the couch as the final waves of his orgasm washed over him. He kissed the back of her sweaty neck and pulled himself out of her with a heavy sigh. He pulled her butt cheeks apart once again and watched with satisfaction as his seed trickled out of her and down her thigh.

"You liked being Daddy's little anal whore, didn't you princess? I bet you're just dying to cum," he said teasingly. Amber nodded, her pussy was still aching with need, and she would give just about anything to be allowed to cum all over Daddy's big cock.

"You should have thought about that before you misbehaved. Now, go clean yourself up. It's time for dinner."

Chapter 14

When she came downstairs, he already had dinner on the table.

"You took your punishment like a good girl. Did you learn your lesson?" She nodded, looking up at him with wide, wet eyes.

"Yes, Daddy," she said meekly.

"Good girl, Daddy is very proud of you." He kissed her on her forehead and pulled out her chair for her to sit. She devoured her dinner, finding that she was ravenously hungry. He watched her with amusement, eating his own dinner slowly. When she sat back with a satisfied sigh, full at last, he was still working his way through his.

"While you were sleeping, I found an open casting call for a local theater group. It's tomorrow at two. You're going," he said with finality. "I printed out the details so you can look over them." She smiled, absolutely amused that he was pretending to be stern when he was doing something incredibly kind, scouring the internet for acting opportunities for her to follow up on.

"Thank you, Daddy," she said, kissing him on the cheek. He continued eating his dinner, steadfastly ignoring the blush that come over his face.

***

She spent the rest of the evening studying lines. She had standard monologue that she usually auditioned with, but she didn't feel like it was appropriate for the dramatic role she was hoping to land. Finally, Malcolm had to drag her away practically.

"Give your brain a rest, little one," he advised. "Come on, let's have a few beers on the couch and then head to bed early. What do you say?" She smiled shyly, knowing that he was right.

She wasn't doing herself any favors by wearing herself out.

"Sounds good, Daddy." Half a beer later, Amber rested her head drowsily on his shoulder as he rubbed her back absentmindedly.

"You have nothing to worry about, little one. You are very talented, and I know that they'll see that and offer you the role right away." The beer was making her head swim, and his light, soothing touch was very relaxing. His warmth emanating through his crisp pressed clothes was oddly comforting, as were his soothing words, and she closed her eyes while he gently explored her body. His fingertips traveled down her legs, tickled her knees, then traced their way back up her tummy and lightly brushing her nipples through her shirt. She nuzzled her face further into his neck to hide her blushing cheeks and giggled quietly, suddenly feeling very shy. Putting his beer down on the coffee table, he cupped her face with his hand and lifted her face so that she had to look at him.

"Don't hide," he whispered. "You're very sexy, kitten." He cupped her breast lightly and chuckled as her cheeks once again turned pink. She held his gaze, though, just as he instructed, her big eyes locked onto his as his hands began to travel downward once more. He dipped his hand between her legs and cupped it against her mound. It radiated with heat as the desire that always seemed to be lying dormant just beneath the surface was beginning to reignite. She gave a tiny little moan and ground her crotch into his palm.

"Poor, needy little baby! You're practically dripping into my hand. Does Daddy's little slut need to cum?" She gasped as he dipped a finger into her slit, overwhelmed by her need for him.

"Yes, Daddy! I need to cum so bad! Please, let me. Please!" The ache that had been building all evening was so great that she didn't care that she was begging. She would beg all night if it brought her the release she needed. He withdrew his finger, slick with her lust, and put it in her mouth.

"Taste how desperate you are, little one.

Suck your juices off Daddy's fingers." Obediently, she suckled, tasting her own sweet nectar, moaning at the taste. He pushed his fingers deeper into her mouth and down her throat, choking her. She gagged, but he only pushed deeper, watching her throat bulge around his intruding digits. As he pulled his hand out, drool dribbled down her lips and chin.

"Does Daddy's greedy little baby want to touch herself?" he asked, teasingly. She felt like she could cum at the slightest stimulation, and the need for release was growing too intense for her to deny any longer.

"Yes, Daddy. Please, may I touch myself? I need it so bad." She pleaded with both her words and her eyes, begging him to end her torture.

"Spread your legs," he commanded sharply. She complied instantly, spreading her legs widely. With her pussy exposed, she waited for his next command.

"You may touch yourself, but you had better not cum until I tell you to." Eagerly, she pressed on her clit, delighting in the delicious waves that washed over her as her finger slipped around her sensitive nub. Her buzz only enhanced the sensations, making her even more attuned to the ecstasy she was providing for herself.

"That's it, kitten," he said, his voice thick with lust. "Now, put one of your fingers inside your tight pussy." With a grunt, she thrust her finger in her dripping folds, pumping it in and out.

"Slow down, greedy. I told you not to cum yet, remember?" Amber whimpered and pouted, but slowed down any way. "That's it, pumpkin." She bit her lip, concentrating on how nice it felt to have her aching pussy get some attention at last. She was already close to the edge, yet her slender finger didn't feel like quite enough anymore after experiencing his thick cock. She thought about how he stretched and filled her and moaned out loud.

"Mmm, good girl. Now touch your clit again." Her finger traveled upwards once more, and she shivered as she pressed against her most sensitive spot. "I know you're dripping wet. I can smell your sweet honey from here. You must really need to cum. Does Daddy's dirty little slut need to cum?" His words made her thrust her hips upwards, excitement coursing through her at the prospect of being allowed a release at last.

"Yes, Daddy. Please let me cum. I need it so bad." Her pace quickened, twirling around her swollen nub and pushing herself dangerously close to the edge.

"Are you close, baby girl?" He leaned closer to her, and she could feel his intense gaze tracking her movements as she obeyed his every command. His breath was heavy against her neck, sending warm tingles all over her body.

"Yes, Daddy. I'm very close. So, so close. Please!" Her voice was starting to take on a whiny quality, but she didn't care. He didn't answer her, only watched her writhe on couch cushions. She could feel her orgasm building. Either she would have to stop touching herself soon, or there would be no stopping it, no matter how hard she tried.

Her legs quivered from the effort of holding herself back, and her soft moans were getting louder and louder.

"Stop!" he growled. Reluctantly, she pulled her hand away. Without thinking, she closed her legs, wanting to feel the pressure of her thighs against her throbbing clit. "Open those legs, baby girl. I'm not done with you yet." Slowly, she extended her legs once again. She clenched her fists by her side, resisting the urge to plunge her fingers back inside of her before he told her to. He watched her for a moment, letting her suffer before sliding his finger into her needy cunt, eliciting a high pitched moan from Amber.

"Is that what Daddy's greedy little slut wanted?" he teased. She couldn't answer in words, so she nodded her head and gripped her thighs. His fingers felt even better than hers. He slipped a second finger inside of her, pumping in and out firmly. "Use your words, pumpkin." Amber bit her lip, her cheeks burning. Her hands released her thighs and covered her face instead.

"Nngh, yes! Daddy's greedy little slut wants to cum. Please, please, please, can I please?" Her words tumbled out rapidly as she grew more and more frantic.

"You're such a good girl. You may cum if you want to, little one." With a cry of relief, Amber threw her head back and surrendered herself to the intense pleasure. Her orgasm broke over her in waves, and she squealed into her hands as her thighs quivered, and her back arched. Hours of sexual tension finally released, Amber sagged back against the couch, but he didn't remove his hand. The climax had made her extra sensitive she instinctively tried to close her legs to block his access but he only slapping her thighs, forcing them open again.

"If you try to close those legs again, I will tie them open again. I already told you, I'm not done with you yet." She whimpered as he continued to fuck her with his fingers, but he was unmoved.

"I thought this is what you wanted, kitten. You were begging to cum just a minute ago. I don't think you've had enough yet." He curled his fingers upwards, seeking the very center of her pleasure. She gasped and bit down on her thumb as his fingers thrust into her with an insistent, unyielding rhythm.

"That's it, sweetie. Be a good little slut and cum for Daddy again." He knew just how and where to touch her to get exactly what he wanted, and within moments, another orgasm was ripping through her, her legs and arms flailing against the overwhelming ecstasy.

"Good girl," he purred, and before she knew it, he was pushing her down onto the couch, his big thick cock pushing into her. For once, he was the impatient one, and he filled her up in one motion. As his girth spread and filled her, she could feel another climax already building.

"You're such a greedy little slut, aren't you? No matter how many times I make you cum, you're still hungry for more." He slammed into her, leaving no part of her untouched as he filled her over and over. Unable to hold back, she came undone on his cock, babbling and thrashing against him as he kept the same steady pace. Each time she came was more intense than the last, each one leaving her even more sensitive to the steady pounding of his cock.

"God, you're so tight, princess. Do you like being a slut for Daddy?"

"Yes, Daddy," she said with a shaky voice. "I love being your slut. Fuck your little slut, Daddy." With a growl, he abandoned his steady rhythm and began fucking her hard and fast. She could feel his cock start to swell and knew that he was close to the edge. As his cock split her open, she could feel one last orgasm mounting.

"Cum inside me, Daddy," she pleaded and gripped his buttocks to pull him deeper inside. "I love it when you give me your cum." He cried out, and as he pumped his hot juices inside of her, she had the most intense pleasure she had ever experienced. Her entire body felt electric, and she was still twitching with ecstasy long after he had stilled inside of her. With a contented sigh, he withdrew, sitting up on the couch. She lay her head down in his lap and he pet her hair while her breath slowly returned to normal.

"Do you see now why Daddy makes you wait sometimes? Wasn't it worth it?" His fingers combed through her hair and massaged her scalp tenderly.

"Yes, Daddy," she said dreamily. "You're always right."

Chapter 15

The next afternoon, Amber practically ran down the sidewalk, bursting with the good news. The elevator seemed even slower than normal, and she tapped her foot impatiently. At last, she burst into the living room where Malcolm was waiting, a nervous expression carved onto his face.

"Well?!" he asked before she could even get her jacket off. "What did they say?" She grinned at him, almost too giddy to get the words out.

"I got it!" she exclaimed. "I got the lead part." His face lit up, and he wrapped her up in a tight bear hug, sweeping her off her feet and swinging her around until she squealed.

"I knew you would," he said smugly as he put her down again. "See, I told you that Daddy is always right. When do you start?"

"Next week," she said. She chewed her lip,

feeling a bit nervous to tell him this next part. "And it's eight shows a week, so I'm afraid it might interfere with my duties as your assistant. I hope that's ok." Suddenly his face got serious. He took her hand and led her over to the couch, motioning for her to sit.

"That's actually something I've been meaning to talk to you about. I'm really glad that you have this acting job to fall back on because I'm afraid that I'm going to have to fire you." Her heart sank as she stared at him in shock. Fired?! Her mind raced, trying to find where she had gone wrong, why he didn't want her anymore. Before she could ask any questions, he continued speaking.

"You see, I want to ask you to be my girlfriend, but you really shouldn't date your employees," She laughed as a wave of relief washed over her, and she slapped his arm, cutting him off.

"That was dirty, Daddy!" she yelled at him between giggles. "You nearly gave me a heart attack, you big meanie." He chuckled, defending himself from her playful swats.

"I surrender, I surrender," he said, pulling her close. "So it that a yes? You'll be my baby girl really and truly?"

"Yes, Daddy," she said, smiling up at him. "I'll be your baby girl really and truly." He kissed her gently, cupping her face lovingly. Even that gentle, loving touch was enough to ignite her desire. She moaned and ran her fingers through his hair, opening her mouth for his tongue.

"What's the matter, princess? Are you starting to feel tingly in your private parts again?" he whispered. They hadn't fucked before her audition, Malcolm said that she should reserve her energy. Now that she was past that hurdle, she was eager to make up for the lost time, even if it was only a few hours. She nodded and bit her lip. "Well, since you've been such a good girl today, I'll let you suck me off." She kneeled in front of him, unzipping his pants to release his monster cock. She took a moment to lovingly nuzzle the cock that she had missed so much all day. He stroked her hair as she wrapped her lips around the tip of his member and swirled her tongue around him, delighting in how his eyes rolled back and a gruff moan escaped his lips. Unable to hold herself back, she swallowed his cock deeply, his member pulsing inside of her tight, warm throat. Pushing past her gag reflex, she worked him in and out of her mouth, swallowing him deeply with every stroke. He gripped her hair, encouraging her to take him faster and deeper, fucking her face with abandon.

"That's a good girl. Make Daddy cum with your mouth, sweetheart." She moaned around his hardness, caressing his balls lightly as she quickened her pace and pushed herself to take him even deeper. As her lips began to graze the very root of his cock, she could feel his testicles tighten, and he pumped his hot jizz deep into her throat, his hands gripping her hair so tightly that it hurt. It was too much for her to swallow, and as he pulled his cock from her mouth, his creamy white cum dribbled out of her mouth and onto her shirt. He chuckled indulgently.

"What a silly, drooly baby you are." He caught some of the jizz that dangled from her chin and fed it back to her, her eager tongue lapping her reward from his salty palms. "I'm tempted to make you wear that cum soaked shirt out tonight so that everyone sees that you're Daddy's spoiled little slave. Say it."

"I'm Daddy's spoiled little slave." She grinned up at him, and he rewarded her with a deep kiss, his tongue lazily her exploring her mouth. "Now get up and show Daddy how wet you are." She stood and proudly lifted her skirt, stepping her feet wide so that he could pull her labia apart and inspect her closely. She was soaking wet from sucking his cock, and the inspection made her pussy tingle all the more.

"Mmm, good girl, I can see you're on your way to being a desperate, drippy mess. Just how I like you. That will have to wait until later. We've got two things to celebrate tonight. Go put on something sexy, baby girl. We're going out tonight."

***

They stumbled back to his apartment sometime later. He had spent the entire night bragging to every stranger that they saw that his girlfriend was going to be a famous actress, something that never failed to make her blush and giggle. They had both drank more than they probably should have, giddy both at her success and their newfound love. Both were reasonably buzzed by the time they got back, so they fumbled with each other's clothes at the same time, giggling and groping each other as they went. Somehow, they managed to get upstairs and into Malcolm's bed. Amber was already most of the way out of her dress, and he jumped at the chance to suck on one of her perky breasts. She moaned at the ripples of pleasure that started at his mouth and ended at her aching pussy. He pulled her dress the rest of the way down as he worked her nipple between his teeth. The pain made her back arch and her folds flooded with desire.

"My dirty girl," he whispered approvingly. He grazed his index finger over her slippery-wet clit. She writhed beneath him and moaned pleadingly. He rolled off of her momentarily, which made her pout. She was even needier and hornier when drunk, it turned out. He chuckled at her neediness and took his pants off, kicking them to the other side of the room. A wicked smile took the place of her pout as she leaned over him, eyeing his cock hungrily. She licked the tip of his hardness and wrapped her lips around him, moaning as she took him further down. She loved how wild with need it made her feel when she asphyxiated herself on his hardness. He pushed himself further down her throat, knowing by now exactly where her limit was and rode the edge as far as he could before pulling her back up by her hair. She managed to take a deep breath before he plunged his cock back into her mouth. He grabbed a fistful of hair and twisted as he thrust into her throat over and over, fucking her face. The pain and domination canceled all thoughts in her head and transformed her into a blank slate of hazy pleasure, eager to serve him for as long as he would let her.

"Touch your pussy," he commanded. She relished the sensation of her velvety smoothness beneath her fingers as she obeyed him. Her fingers traveled easily over her wet pussy, exploring her clit and hungry hole. He jammed his cock hard down her throat and held it there while she gagged and choked. She plunged two fingers into her cunt and fucked herself wildly. Even two fingers weren't enough to satisfy her anymore, however. What she needed was Malcolm. He couldn't hold himself back anymore and let himself unload down her throat. She eagerly swallowed his seed and giggled as she wiped away some that had dripped out onto her lips.

"Your turn," he growled, pushing her back

onto the bed and diving between her legs.

"Thank you, Daddy," she moaned and spread her legs eagerly for him.

"I love the way you eat my pussy." He leaned down and gently pressed his lips against her slick folds. For a moment, he merely breathed her in, savoring the fresh scent and heat of her arousal. Amber had never felt so sexy as she did when he used her like that. He made her feel so exposed and vulnerable yet quivering with electric anticipation. His tongue dove into her folds, intimately familiar by now with every inch of her, knowing all of her most sensitive spots. His tongue was so warm, so wet, and he seemed to delight in teasing her until her entire body felt like it was burning with lust. His strong hands gripped her thighs and held her legs open. She writhed and moaned beneath him, gasping "Daddy!" over and over as her arousal built. He pulled her swollen clit into his mouth, flicking it with his tongue. She buried her sweaty, trembling fingers in his hair instead, drawing him closer.

"Fuck, Daddy! That feels so good!" Her thighs tried to close around him, but he merely dug his fingers deeper into her flesh and kept them pinned in place. Her feeble efforts were no match for his strength, and that realization, along with the dull pain from his grip, pushed her closer to her climax. She loved how helpless he made her feel.

"Please, Daddy. May I pretty please cum? You feel so good, Daddy!" she pleaded, gripping his shoulders as she held herself back and waited for his permission. He didn't answer her at first. Instead, he plunged two fingers into her slit and pumped them in and out of her while he continued to tongue her clit. It took every ounce of her willpower not to explode then and there. Every one of her muscles clenched as she rode the edge of climax, determined to wait like a good girl until he gave her permission. Her obedience was soon rewarded.

"You may cum now," he whispered against her before pressing his tongue into her clit once more. She finally succumbed to the waves of pleasure that had been building up, her body convulsing as she gripped him by the hair and rode his tongue to orgasm. He growled with satisfaction, quickening his pace, wanting to completely overwhelm her with pleasure. Her muscles at last unclenched and she lay panting and shivering.

"You taste so good, pumpkin," he murmured and nuzzled her inner thighs as she recovered from her intense experience. His kisses began to travel upwards, across her firm tummy, up her ribcage, around her breasts, and up her neck. Their lips met, his tongue intertwined with hers. Nestled between her legs, she could feel that he was already hard again. With a grunt, he grabbed her hand and guided it to his hardness, shivering slightly as she gripped him.

"You see what you do to Daddy, little girl?" he rasped, his voice thick with lust. "That's because you're so, so sexy." She stroked him, delighting in the way it made his brow wrinkle and his breath to get ragged. He buried his face in her neck, kissing and licking her neck while she played with his member, her hands exploring his hardness, his balls, his everything, so happy to have him for her very own. As his excitement grew, so did hers, and she was once again consumed by an untamed desire. She longed to have his cock inside of her and rubbed his swollen head against her silky, wet folds. He grunted and grabbed a fistful of her hair, making her groan in response. She guided him to her slick opening, and he pressed in slowly. Her fingers dug into his buttocks as he inched his length inside of her. Once he was completely sheathed inside of her, she felt all of her inhibitions melting away.

"Oh, Daddy. Fuck me! Fuck me hard, please!" she cried out and pulled his hips closer. He began to move inside of her, the walls of her pussy hugging him so tight it was hard not release himself deep in her wetness. He twisted his fist in her hair and pumped into her. She began squealing and babbling, her mind and body totally awash with the intense pleasure of his thick cock spreading her, filling her up so deep, his hardness driving into her needy core. He pressed his forehead into hers and pinned her wrists against the bed, enjoying the feeling of possessing her completely.

"You're mine, baby girl. All. Mine." He punctuated his words with hard thrusts into her hot tightness. Her eyes rolled back, and she continued to stutter incoherently. Occasionally, he could make out the words "fuck" and "yes" and "Daddy" but she mostly seemed beyond words, beyond thought, consumed instead with pure animalistic hunger.

"You're doing such a good job, baby," he said huskily. "You're being such a good slut for Daddy, letting him use your tight little pussy. I'm so proud of you, little one." Amber came again, even harder than before, his dirty words filling her with a delicious heat that permeated throughout her entire being and left her shivering and quaking. He rutted his hips against hers, realizing that he wouldn't be able to hold back much longer as her orgasm made her grip him even tighter.

"Daddy's going to cum inside you, Princess. I'm going to fill you up, baby. Here it comes." His cock twitched, and he couldn't hold back a shuddering grunt as he pumped his hot, sticky seed inside of her. Collapsing into a sweaty, trembling mess, he lay panting against her neck as she caressed his hair and kissed his salty forehead. After a moment, he withdrew from her and scooped her up into his arms, kissing her deeply.

"You're such a good girl," he whispered silkily into her hair and wrapped her tightly in his arms. "I'm so lucky to have you." She relaxed into the safety of his arms, wrapped up in a cocoon of hazy contentment. He held her until her eyes began to get heavy once again. When it was apparent that she was falling asleep, he pulled the covers over them and kissed her on the forehead.

"I love you, Amber," he whispered in her ear, his voice trembling as he said it.

"I love you too, Daddy," she murmured sleepily, wrapping her arms tightly around his neck.

Chapter 16

Amber officially moved in with Malcolm right away and signed her lease over to Leslie's co-worker. She let the girl take the pick of her furniture and sold the rest, not seeing much point in putting it in storage. Malcolm told her not to worry about pitching in for rent, which was a relief. She didn't know exactly how much he paid, but from the look of his apartment, there was no way she could ever afford it. Thanks to his generosity, she was able to pay Leslie back the money she owed her which was a huge relief to Amber. Leslie had been so kind to her when they were roommates, and she deserved to have that kindness repaid. The play ran much longer than expected, selling out every night for weeks on end. Many of the reviews singled her out by name, giving her credit for the success of the show. After struggling for so long for a breakthrough, it was amazingly gratifying to see her name in print at last. Every night, Malcolm was right in the front row, silently cheering her on. Even when the show was extended and he had seen the show enough times to know it by heart, he was still right there, looking just as proud of her as he had the first night. The final evening of the show, Malcolm gave her a giant bouquet of flowers as the crowd gave her a standing ovation. It was so gratifying to have the man she loved supporting her as she achieved her dreams. It was one of the many reasons why she loved him so much. It was late when she finally said all of her goodbyes and graciously accepted all of her congratulations. They decided to walk home that evening, wanting to enjoy the lovely, warm evening and get some fresh air. He wrapped his arm around her waist as they walked and talked, occasionally stopping to look at the window displays in the shops. It was the first time she had gotten just to enjoy the city since she moved there and she was glad that she was seeing it with him.

"I'm so proud of you, baby girl," he said and squeezed her tightly. "You looked so beautiful up there on that stage. You're definitely going to be a star after this, I just know it." She blushed but hoped that he was right. *Daddy's always right;* she reminded herself and smiled.

"Thank you, Daddy," she said and sniffed her bouquet, remembering how fun the entire experience was and how she couldn't wait to do it again. She didn't need to be a star, not really, but she did hope that she gained a good enough reputation to maintain steady work. Eventually, they passed an alley, and Malcolm slowed his pace. He looked cautiously down the alley, making sure that it was completely empty before looking at her with a naughty glint in his eye. She recognized the look and immediately knew what was on his mind. He loved fucking her in public, and she loved to let him. He took her by the hand and pulled her toward the alley. She looked over her shoulder to make sure that no one saw and followed him, already feeling a tingle between her legs. Once they were in the shadows, he stood behind her and began to run his hands over her curves. She leaned into him, eager for him already.

"You really did look beautiful up there, kitten," he whispered in her ear. She moaned and ground her ass against his crotch, delighting in the way it made him sigh. "You're the sexiest woman in the world. You know that?" She nodded, knowing that in his mind, it was true. He was always telling her how beautiful and sexy he found her, always telling her that she was the woman of his dreams and she never got tired of hearing.

"Good girl," he growled. "Now pull up your skirt." Her clit was throbbing as she did what he commanded, her shaking hands pulled her skirt up over the swell of her ass, exposing herself to the dim light of the alleyway. She faced the wall and waited, her skin tingling with anticipation. He knew how much waiting made her crazy, which was why he delayed her pleasure so frequently.

"Now pull down your panties," he

commanded next. Eagerly, she pulled down her thong, her pussy already aching for him. As he groped her bare ass, she heard the sound of metal on metal as he unzipped his pants, and she moaned, knowing what was coming next.

"Bend over," he said. She put her hand on the wall to steady herself and bent at the hips, giving him a full view of her pussy and ass. She loved showing off for him, loved the hungry look he always got for her. He made a satisfied noise and began running his cock along her crack. She moaned and thrust her hips back, craving to have his thick cock inside of her.

"You want to be fucked in a back alley like some dirty little slut, little one?" He pressed his hard cock against her clit as he teased her, making her legs tremble slightly. He laughed as he tapped it against her slick folds, making her jump and twitch with every tap. She nearly yelped at the sensation but bit her lip and stayed quiet lest she spoiled their game by getting caught.

"Oh kitten, you're already so wet and needy

for Daddy's cock. You just can't get enough of it, can you?" She shook her head and groaned, squirming back against him. It was true. They fucked constantly yet she still craved him nearly all of the time.

"No, Daddy, I can never get enough of your cock. I need you to fuck me, please."

"Good girl," he sighed, inching himself into her slowly. Her eyes rolled back in her head as he slowly filled her, burying himself in her completely. He held her there for a moment, grabbing her by the hips as he savored the feeling of being so deep inside of her. As he pulled out, he deliberately keeping his pace as slow as possible to drive her crazy. Amber whimpered quietly as he slowly stretched her open, pleasuring her but also leaving her aching for more. She thrust her hips back in an attempt to increase the tempo, but he only slapped her ass to keep her in line.

"Slow down, little one," he warned. "Don't want you getting too excited. I know how loud you can get, and we don't want the whole world to know that you're a dirty little slut who likes to get fucked in back alleys, now do we?" Her pussy tightened around him, his words only making her crave him all the more. She couldn't deny that she could get quite loud indeed, especially when he said dirty things like that to her. She whined and gripped the wall as he fucked her in his own sweet time, seemingly not the least bit concerned that they could be discovered at any moment even with her being quiet.

"I'll be quiet, Daddy," she promised. "Please fuck me harder." He made a strangled noise and slammed his cock into her, suddenly pounding fast and hard, no more teasing. She held on tight, biting her lip to keep from screaming. Every thrust sent a lightning bolt of pleasure through her, and all she was aware of was how much she loved the dirty things he did to her and how good it felt to be his and his alone.

"Good girl," he whispered. "That's a good little slut." Suddenly, he was pulsing inside of her, grunting as he pumped her full of his seed. It felt so amazing, the way he filled her up, her reward for a job well done. She felt like she would never get enough of his hot cum, no matter how many times they fucked. As he pulled out of her, he was careful to catch all the semen that dripped out onto her panties as he pulled them up. He pulled her against him, wrapping one arm around her waist as he kissed her from behind. She squeezed her thighs together, savoring the warm sensation.

"That was perfect, baby girl. You're so sexy." He wrapped his arms around her, holding her close. She was still aching for him, but she closed her eyes contentedly, enjoying the hunger. It made her feel so alive and so sexy. He took her by the hand, leading her back to the sidewalk. As they walked home, she had a reminder of who she belonged to with every step.

Chapter 17

That evening, as she was getting ready for bed, she noticed that he was watching her more closely than usual.

"What is it?" she asked, finally, after catching him staring at her for the third time.

"What do you think you'd like to do now that the play is over?" he asked thoughtfully. She shrugged, caught off guard by the question.

"I don't really have a plan," she said. "I'll probably start auditioning for another role as soon as I can."

"Why don't you take some time off?" he suggested. "I'll take some time off, too, and we can take a trip somewhere."

"Seriously?" she asked, seriously considering it. "Where would we go? It was his turn to shrug as though he hadn't considered that part yet.

"Anywhere you like. Someplace tropical? The mountains, maybe?" She considered it quietly for a moment as she brushed her hair. Her head had been so wrapped up in getting her acting career going these past few years that she had never considered what kind of vacation she might like to take, and it took her a while to come to a decision.

"Someplace tropical sounds nice," she said finally. "How about Jamaica?" He grinned and nodded, getting excited at the idea.

"That's perfect. I've never been so we can both experience it for the first time together."

"I like the sound of that," she said, putting down her brush and joining him in the bed.

"Good," he said. "I'll start making the arrangements right away." She sighed and stretched, then cuddled up against him, so that he was spooning her from behind. Cuddling in that position never failed to make him horny, and tonight was no different. He brushed his fingertips lightly over her nipples, and she could feel him already getting hard against the warm swell of her buttocks. She began to grind her butt cheeks against him, already whimpering and squealing as he pinched her nipples harder, delighting in the way her eyes rolled back in her head with the heady mixture of pain and pleasure.

"I love what a greedy slut you are," he growled into her ear, one hand sliding up from her breast to her throat. He didn't apply any pressure, just held her against him like that, letting them both relish the feeling of control. After a moment, she began to squirm impatiently against him, trying to provoke a response. He tightened his hand on her throat, a tiny gasp escaping her lips. Without another word, he plunged his hard cock deep in her tight pussy, still slick with his semen, and grinned as she winced in pain and pleasure. For her, the two were inseparable now, and she yearned towards him, eager for more. He tightened his grip on her throat, delighting in the way her pussy tightened around him, and she rolled her eyes back in her head.

"That's it, baby girl. Show Daddy how dirty you like it." She tried to moan, but it came out as a muted squeak, her air-restricted by the large meaty hand wrapped around her neck. He fucked her harder, moving her hand to her clit. "Show Daddy how much you love getting fucked." She rubbed at her clit furiously, squeaking and squirming, working herself up to a climax. As he sensed she was getting close, he suddenly withdrew and released her throat, leaving her gasping and quivering.

"Not yet, kitten." He slapped her hard on the ass, leaving behind a bright pink handprint. He liked the look of it so much that he left half a dozen more, as she yelped in vain. Once again, he was overwhelmed with the feeling of being incredibly lucky to be with a woman so sexy and insatiable. She was the first woman he had ever been who could keep up with his sexual appetites and then some. "Suck Daddy's cock." The eagerness on her face as she turned herself around and sought out his erection with plump, pink lips took his breath away. As her hot mouth engulfed him, she moaned around his shaft, making him shiver with delight. He ran his fingers through her soft hair, and he sank his cock deeper into her mouth. By now, she was well trained in the art of deepthroating, so he went deeper. Once he hit her limit, she gagged but continued to pleasure him, undeterred.

"Yes, that's it. You're making Daddy's cock feel so good." She let herself get lost in pleasuring him, her favorite activity. He continued to mumble encouragement to her, wrapping her in a cocoon of safety and trust. She loved being a vessel for his pleasure, being able to express her love for him in such a tangible, physical way. She felt like she could suck his cock for hours, happily lost in a daze of submissive servitude. All too soon, however, he pulled her up from his cock by her hair. He kissed her passionately and deeply, pulling and twisting her nipples mercilessly. She writhed against him, seeking out his hardness with her aching hole, silently begging to be filled. He could sense her neediness and decided to toy with it, rubbing the head of his hard penis against her tender clit as he continued to twist and pinch her nipples. The combination turned her into a moaning, desperate thing, no longer capable of clear thought, only a bottomless pit of need that only he could fulfill. As she began to babble incoherently, lost in a fog of lust and submission, he guided her to sit on his cock, filling her at last. She sighed with deep satisfaction as he sank into her, and she wrapped her arms around his neck tightly, wanting to be even closer still. He guided her hips with his hands, and she began to ride him with abandon. He lie back, enjoying the sight of his beloved naked and uninhibited, her long hair flowing over her alabaster skin as she brought them both to the brink of ecstasy.

"Do you like that? Do you want to cum on Daddy's cock, baby girl?" he asked, already knowing the answer. He grabbed her buttocks with both hands and forced her down on his throbbing erection, filling her so deeply and completely that she almost did cum without his permission. Quivering with barely contained ecstasy, she managed to nod her head and squeak out, "Yes, Daddy." He put his thumb on her clit and thrust into her again and again, loving keeping her right on the threshold. She was so beautiful and sexy. He never wanted to stop fucking her. When he felt like he could no longer hold himself back, he gave her the command.

"Cum for me, little one." She moaned with relief, gripping his hips with her thighs and his cock with her pussy as she finally let herself go, let the climax that had been steadily building wash over. As she shook and cried out, she could feel his cock twitch as he flooded her with his hot seed. They held onto each other as the electric waves of their mutual orgasm receded, and they lie panting and sweating, tangled in one another as they slowly came back to reality. She suddenly started giggling, not even sure what was funny but so full of effervescent joy that it was spilling out of her. Much to her surprise, he too started laughing, burying his face in her neck as he held her tight against him as their bodies shook with mirth. After a moment, he kissed her gently and slid her off of him and onto the bed. Soon, they would drift off to sleep together, gathering their energy to face the world once more, side by side. For now, they were safe and content in their love nest.

Who is Tina Moore?

Tina Moore has enjoyed the lifestyle of a Mommy Domme for several years. She began exploring kink and BDSM in her youth and found her love of being a strict Mommy Domme in early 2000. Tina Moore is now an author of many MDLG, DDLG and ABDL themed novels.

Follow her on:

Author Page on Amazon

Instagram @tinamoore.kdp